Tea shop owner and pastry chef Bailey Willis is nonplussed when she finds a handsome Texan sprawled out on the floor of A Spot of Tea. Trevor Anderson, on the other hand, is instantly smitten. Some might call him a broken-down cowboy, but that doesn't mean he cannot pursue a beautiful woman, even if she is a northerner and a Green Bay Packers fan!

Unfortunately, Bailey has other things on her mind, like winning the Hales Corners, WI holiday bake-off. When Trevor provides a valuable assist, Bailey regards him in a different light. Too bad he's planning to head back to his ranch after the new year. Will Bailey agree to wear Trevor's Texas-size ring? Will Trevor agree to settle in the frozen tundra, the site of one of the Dallas Cowboys' most humiliating defeats? Hold on to your cowboy hat, folks, this tale of romance will take you for a ride. Texas style!

Broken Down Cowboy
Copyright © 2023 Seelie Kay
ISBN: 978-1-4874-4012-1
Cover art by Martine Jardin

Published by eXtasy Books Inc

Look for us online at:
www.eXtasybooks.com

Broken Down Cowboy

By

Seelie Kay

DEDICATION

For every middle-aged woman who ever dreamed of finding her own cowboy, one with a little seasoning!

CHAPTER ONE: A SNAP IN HER GARTERS!

Bailey Willis carefully balanced a three-tier stand filled with scones, pastries, finger sandwiches, and other sweet treats. She then pushed through the split kitchen door.

She passed her assistant, Jilly, who stood at attention in a proper English maid uniform in front of the elegant dining room. "Afternoon tea at table five. Bring the tea cart, please."

Jilly smiled. "Sure thing, boss. I'll even bring the sugar, milk, lemon, and clotted cream."

Bailey rolled her eyes. "Watch the sass, sweetheart." She winked at Jilly to show she was joking and moved toward table five. When she arrived, she saw a grandmother and her two granddaughters dressed to the nines for a formal tea party. Absently, she wondered whether the two girls actually enjoyed being dressed up in all that lace and frills. At their age, she'd hated it. Mostly she'd dressed in jeans and tee shirts. Gently, Bailey settled the stand in the middle of the table.

Most of their patrons grabbed at the delicacies before fixing their tea, but Millicent Franklin was a stickler for protocol. Bailey knew she preferred to pour and then serve her grandchildren cakes, one at a time. She smiled as Jilly approached with the tea cart.

Jilly curtsied and asked in a clipped British accent, "And who shall be Mother today?"

Mrs. Franklin smiled. "I think it's Lisa's turn, and she's

been practicing." The woman gazed fondly at the two children.

"Very good, ma'am." Jilly stepped back from the cart and stood at parade rest.

Ten-year-old Lisa rose from the table, went to the tea cart, inspected its contents carefully, and nodded with approval. She turned to her grandmother and in a soft voice, asked, "How would you like your tea today, Grandmother?"

"Two sugars and a quick splash of cream, please."

Lisa carefully placed the sugar cubes in a teacup, added some cream, and filled the cup with their chosen tea. She set the cup on a saucer and placed it in front of her grandmother. She turned to her older sister. "Mallory, may I serve you tea?"

Mallory smoothed the pink cloth napkin on her lap and smiled sweetly. "Yes, please. Just a hint of milk for me, sister. I so enjoy a cuppa lavender tea. I don't want to dilute the flavor."

Jilly bit her lip and squelched a giggle.

Bailey knew Jilly always found the younger patrons entertaining. But a break from character would impact the formality of tea. And that formality was what made Bailey's tea shop, *A Spot of Tea*, special. Bailey shot Jilly a stern look, and she sobered. Her caramel-toned face and brown-green eyes settled into a more deferential expression.

Lisa quickly placed the teacup before her sister and then prepared her own. She returned to her seat and gazed at her grandmother expectantly.

Mrs. Franklin smiled proudly. "Very nice, Lisa. Now what will you have? I believe our sandwiches are date cream cheese, chicken salad, and cucumber. Our scones are walnut, lemon blueberry, and some sort of other dessert scone." She cocked an eyebrow at Jilly.

Jilly stepped forward. "Those are triple chocolate, ma'am."

Mrs. Franklin nodded. "And the cakes are as I requested?"

She gazed at Bailey.

"Yes, ma'am. Sunshine cake, lemon poppyseed, and a strawberry torte."

Before Mrs. Franklin could respond, they heard a loud crash, and then the sound of breaking glass. The floor seemed to shake.

Bailey paled and quickly curtsied. "Excuse me, please." She hurried back into the kitchen where her chef, Spencer, held a substantial pastry brush and was swatting a man sprawled out on the floor. A black cowboy hat sat at the man's feet. "Spencer, what the devil? We do not beat on our customers." She extended an arm to the man and helped him to his feet. "Now, will someone please explain to me what's going on?"

Spencer's victim picked up his hat and slapped it on his leg, then reshaped the crown. He placed the hat on his head. His soft brown eyes, punctuated by crow's feet that appeared carved into his tan face, gazed at Bailey, and his full lips curled up in a cocky grin. "Sorry, ma'am," he drawled in a sexy baritone. "I didn't mean to disturb you, but my daughter sent me to pick up her order for my granddaughter's birthday party. I saw how crowded it was out front, so I thought it best to come 'round to the back door." He made a face. "Not sure how I wound up on the floor. Guess I slipped." He shrugged and chuckled. "Guess that happens to those of us ready for the pasture."

Bailey squelched a sigh. *Pasture my eye.* He couldn't be more than fifty, around her age. This guy could be on the cover of a romance novel. He was tall and sturdy, with curly dark hair, bushy eyebrows, and just a hint of a five o'clock shadow. And that voice. She could just imagine the man whispering into her ear after a night of passionate sex. A tiny shiver raced up and down her spine. She was exiting her forties, but her body was not immune to a handsome cowboy.

Damn, he was fine.

Spencer planted his hands on his skinny hips and scowled. "He didn't knock. He just whipped open the door and barged on in. Scared the bejesus out of me. I dropped a water glass." He shot the cowboy a dirty look. "His boots must be wet, because he took a less-than-graceful tumble. You know, ass over teakettle? You may be all that in Texas, cowboy. But in Wisconsin, we wipe our feet before entering a building." He clucked his tongue and tossed his head. "Everyone knows what happens when you track in snow."

The cowboy held up his hands and tried to squelch a grin. "Hey, I apologize. In my defense, I knocked several times. When no one responded, I just thought it would be easier to come in . . . "

"Oh, for Pete's Sake. Did you grow up in a barn?" Spencer huffed. "I need to go clean up. I've got enough flour on me to enter a powder puff derby." He flounced away, muttering about uncouth cowboys with bull crap on their boots.

Bailey rolled her eyes and giggled. She smiled at the man. "I hope that pastry brush didn't seriously injure you."

The man chortled. "I'm a bit buttered up, but it beats my granddaughter's fingerpaints all over my face. As long as he doesn't force me into an oven, I think I'll be fine." He held out a hand. "Trevor Anderson. Here to pick up an order for Beverly Gaines."

Bailey took his hand and shook it. "Bailey Willis." She jutted her chin toward the hallway. "That screwball's boss." She smiled. "He's a bit dramatic, but his pastries are divine, so we tolerate him. Let me get your order." She opened the doors to a large stainless-steel refrigerator and walked in. She returned with a large square box and set it on the counter.

"Let me get that for you, darlin'. That's too big for a tiny filly like you." Trevor touched her shoulder and nuzzled her aside.

That simple touch almost sent Bailey into an orgasm-induced meltdown. Damn, had it been that long since a sexy man touched her? *Don't embarrass yourself, woman. He's a customer and won't be back.* She snorted. "If I can lift one-hundred-pound bags of flour, I assure you I can handle a cake box." She hip-checked him. "Now, out of my way."

Trevor's eyes widened. "Oh, you're a feisty one." He gently picked her up, moved her away from the counter, and grabbed the box. "Ma'am, I may be a broken-down cowboy from Texas, but I'll be damned if I'll make a *purty* lady like you lift boxes I can handle myself. That just isn't right."

Bailey heard a big sigh and turned to stare at Spencer.

He had his hands crossed over his heart, grinning like a cat who'd caught a mouse. "Oh, isn't that sweet? A real gentleman." His smile quickly dissolved. "Since you're being so helpful and all, there's a broom in the corner. Mind sweeping up that broken glass over there? Maybe mop the floor?"

Bailey glared at him. "We do not ask customers to serve as janitors, Spence. As I recall, the bakers keep the kitchen clean." She cocked her head. "Unless you'd like to be demoted, I suggest you do your job." Bailey pointed out the back door and smiled at Trevor. "I'll help you get that to your vehicle. Please be careful, that alley is slippery. Snow and freezing temps do not mix well in this climate." She opened the back door and motioned he should follow.

Carefully, Trevor grasped the box and stepped around Spencer. He went through the door and pointed at a large pickup truck, complete with a set of horns on the front end.

Bailey's mouth dropped open. "Are those horns real?"

Trevor chuckled. "Yes, ma'am. Those belonged to one of my Longhorn females, old Betsy Lou. She wandered off the pasture and got into a tangle with a drunk cowboy on a county highway. I saved the horns, but Betsy Lou lost the battle." He made a face. "They tickle my granddaughters, so I brought them with me this trip."

She shook her head. "Best you lock those down tight. We have enough problems with car thieves around here. That set of horns will be just too tempting."

"As my daughter has already informed me." Trevor shrugged. "But I'm only here for a couple of weeks, leaving after New Year's. I'll be parking my truck in a garage, mostly. Guess I'll take my chances." He turned a full-watt smile on Bailey, and she tried not to swoon. Darn, he was only here for the holidays? That sucked. With an inner sigh, Bailey helped Trevor position the cake box in his back seat and waved as he pulled away.

Well, that woman certainly had some snap in her garters!

Trevor smiled. "Never expected to meet such a looker up here in the Ice Bowl." He shivered. "Who lives up here anyway? It's darn near ten degrees, and there's ice everywhere. If I'm not careful, I'm gonna lose a hip." The NFL Championship game in the late seventies saw the Packers and the Cowboys face off. Known as the Ice Bowl, it was a memory that few Dallas Cowboys fans had let go of. The game was played in Green Bay, where the temperature hovered at minus thirteen, with a wind chill of minus forty-eight.

His granddaddy was fit to be tied when the Packers won by four points at the tail end of the game. Until the day he died, he claimed it was a set-up and horribly unfair. "No corn-bred Texan could survive in those temperatures, much less win a football game. We were far better than the Packers and everyone knew it. But we were a new team and Lombardi was king, so the fix was in. Not sure how they froze us out that day, but there's a lesson there. Never trust the Green Bay Packers or their fans. They're dirty."

Trevor sighed. Granddaddy had probably spun in his grave when little Bevvy marched north on the arm of a Yank, despite his protestations. At first, he had been skeptical. He would have bet she'd be back within a month, or at least after the first cold spell. But Bevvy was stubborn, been that way since she was a child. Like her momma, it was Bevvy's way or the highway. Trevor snorted. His wife had passed a decade ago and, in that time, his only daughter had tightened the noose around his heart and his wallet. She knew how to sweet talk him, much to the chagrin of his two sons. They'd even made him a tee shirt that read, *No one says no to Bevvy, especially Daddy.* But turnabout was fair play, and his teasing had been merciless when Bevvy suckered his boys out of a full-length fur coat one Christmas.

Admittedly, Bevvy, though spoiled rotten, was also a bright light that drew people to her like a mosquito to a swamp. Even her husband, the esteemed Dr. William Gaines, indulged her every whim. That guy was running with the big hogs. Bevvy wanted for nothing. Trevor chuckled. She might have her husband under her thumb, but his two grandchildren were giving her a run for her money. It was like trying to herd 'coons with a butterfly net.

That was why Bevvy had pleaded with him to travel to Yankee country to corral the young 'uns while she prepared for the holidays. For the next few weeks, he was a boot-scootin' nanny. But his meetin' with the adorable Bailey Willis might just compensate. Who knew a snow bunny could be so attractive? Blondes rarely drew him, but this one had something special. She was elegant. Yeah, that was the word. Elegant. And confident, with sharp blue eyes that glowed with intelligence. But she wasn't stuffy or snobby like some of the other beautiful women he knew. She was funny and without pretense. That tiny compact body was the real kicker. Despite the chef's coat, Bailey Willis has curves in all the right places. Curves he could hang on to.

He peered at his blue tooth screen as his phone rang, then

groaned. Bevvy. Again. Reluctantly, he swiped at the Blue-Tooth button on his driving wheel and grumbled, "Yes, my darling daughter. How may I serve you?"

"Oh, Daddy, don't be so grumpy," Bevvy tittered. "You know, I appreciate everything you've been doing for me. Besides, you said you needed a break from the ranch, so I'm giving you one." She muffled the phone and told someone to wash their hands. He hoped it was a child. "Anyway, I'm so glad I caught you. I plum forgot to pick up the gift bags for Evie's party."

"Seems to me that the only person who should receive gifts is my adorable granddaughter, the one celebrating her birthday."

Beverly giggled. "Oh, Daddy, up here, they give out gift bags at every opportunity. Some big, some small, but half the time people go to parties just for gifts. As Billy says, usually the food stinks and the booze is bottom shelf, but the parting gifts are usually worth it."

Trevor rolled his eyes. "The free food and drink aren't enough? Damn Yankees. Always trying to squeeze blood out of a turnip. Everyone knows there's no blood in a damn turnip, but those bozos keep trying."

Beverly laughed. "I wouldn't say that out loud around here, Daddy. People might take offense. They're still miffed about the last time the Cowboys beat the Packers. They hate the Cowboys almost as much as they hate the Bears."

Trevor harrumphed. "The feeling's mutual, but when you're a few sandwiches short of a picnic, I guess I can excuse a little jealousy." Besides, good old Dr. Gaines had a skybox at Lambeau Field that he shared with a few colleagues. He had been kind enough to invite Trevor and his sons up for some games with the Cowboys. Hell, Trevor had even met a few players thanks to Billy, like that quarterback who'd defected to the Jets and the guy with the shampoo commercial.

"Noted. Now, what am I picking up and where?"

"Well, there's this cute little gift shop on Highway One Hundred, which is also called Lover's Lane. Just look for Forest Home. It's at that cross-section." She repeated the name. "Now, you are getting twelve bags with a balloon decoration for the kids and twelve more that are metallic gold for the mothers. I'm texting you what should be in the bags. Make sure you check each bag before you pay."

Oh, Lordy. "Am I footing the bill, too?"

"Oh, Daddy. Everyone knows you've got more money than a gold-plated rooster. It can be your gift to Evie."

"I already got her a fancy new bike."

Beverly snorted. "It's not like you bought her a sports car. That might set you back."

His phone pinged with a text. Trevor sighed. "I'm headed there now. But when I get back, you and I need to have a little chat."

"About what, Daddy?"

"That purty little filly at the tea shop. The one named Bailey. Hair like sunshine and eyes the color of a tropical sea? And a smart businesswoman to boot."

For once, Bevvy was silent. Then she cooed, "Well, she *is* around your age, in her late forties, I'd guess. Everyone loves her. She's just so sweet." Bevvy's voice switched to a conspiratorial tone. "I heard she used to be a lawyer, but one day, she and the women at her firm just up and quit because of poor treatment." She squealed, "Oh, Daddy. Was it love at first sight?"

"Oh, for goodness' sake, I just wanna ask you a few questions about her. She may give me sweet dreams tonight, but that doesn't mean I'm gonna marry her."

Bevvy blubbered, "Oh, Daddy, that makes me so happy. You need a little kick in your step, and Bailey is the one to give it to you. We have to make a plan. Once Mom died, you kind of lost your edge, but Billy and I will set you right. Now pick up those gift bags and run home. We have a party in two hours. Then we'll talk."

"Yes, sir."

Bevvy chuckled and ended the call.

Trevor was a bit surprised at the excitement that coursed through him. Not because of Evie's party, which would be over the top to be sure, but because he'd just committed to wooing a beautiful lady he actually liked. One that had fire. Wisconsin was cold, a frozen tundra, but maybe Bailey Willis was the key to stayin' warm at night.

Chapter Two: The Cake

Bailey glared at the chocolate cake on the counter. Dammit, where was the peppermint?

For the past week, she had been experimenting with recipes for a Chocolate Peppermint Whipped Cream Cake. It should have been easy to make. Add some peppermint extract, then a crushed peppermint stick or two, and stir. Unfortunately, it didn't taste like the cake she was trying to duplicate, the one she'd had in a London tearoom. Every recipe she'd tried was too minty or not minty enough. What was she doing wrong?

Jilly swept into the kitchen and grinned. "That dastardly chocolate peppermint cake, again?" She snickered. "You're running out of time if you want to enter the Christmas bake-off. What's the matter? Did that handsome cowboy throw you off your game?"

Bailey continued to stare at the cake. Jilly hip-checked her, startling her. "Er, what?" She made a face. "What's this about a cowboy?"

Jilly laughed. "Boy, you really are out of it. Is it lust or the cake?"

Bailey made a face. "Sure, the guy was hot, but he's only here for the holidays. Besides, this cake is my priority. I need to win this contest. I'm still recovering from the pandemic slump. I need to pull in more income. Business is good, but it could always be better. I want every single person in Milwaukee County to come to my tea shop for a taste of my Chocolate Peppermint Whipped Cream Cake. If I win the bake-off, I can make that happen. I wish I could figure out what I'm doing wrong." She screwed up her nose. "I'm missing something."

"Well, in my experience, adding a little booze to a cake works wonders. Did you try that?"

"Not sure I can serve a liquor cake to kids." She gazed at Jilly. Today, the young woman had somehow woven red and green crystals into her corn rows. She looked like a Christmas tree.

Jilly sighed. "Yeah, but kids aren't judging the bake-off. Adults are. And if you win, you could always find a non-alcoholic substitute. Too bad, though. My gran used to dump a little brandy in our milk when we slept over. We passed out as soon as our heads hit the pillow, which I'm sure was her intention. She snickered. "Now that would be a great selling point. Try our liquor cake. Guaranteed to knock your kids out at bedtime."

Bailey rolled her eyes. "Get back to work, sweetheart. I imagine we have a few hungry customers out there."

Jilly swiped at her braids and sighed. She walked into the refrigerator and returned with a tray of scones. "Some woman just walked in and asked for four dozen scones for her office. Picky little bitch. She only wants lemon blueberry. I tried to convince her to go with a mix, but she's not budging."

Bailey groaned. "That will wipe us out before afternoon tea, and I don't have a substitute."

Jilly flashed an evil grin. "Can I send her on her way? Tell her we can't accommodate her?" She folded her hands and batted her eyelashes. "Please? I told her we're not a bakery, that we just sell our baked goods to accompany tea. She wasn't having it. Got all snooty."

"Nope. Business is business. I'll just have to call Spence in early to whip up a substitute." She frowned. "Maybe we need to require pre-orders for more than a dozen of one item. Last-minute orders like that just mess things up."

Jilly nodded. "We require reservations for the tea parties, don't see why we can't ask for twenty-four-hours-notice on large orders?"

Bailey sighed. "Well, tell her, politely, that we can accommodate her today, but only because she beat the lunch rush. In the future, we'd appreciate an advance order."

Jilly huffed. "Doubt she will bother. She's the type who'd place a big order, then forget to pick it up."

"Which is why we will request a deposit."

"Oh, yeah." Jilly pulled out a pastry box and started assembling it. She taped the sides, then carefully filled it with scones, counting as she went along. "No baker's dozen for you," she muttered. "Only pre-orders get that." She scowled at the box. "Grrrrrr."

Bailey backed into the kitchen with a tray piled high with dirty dishes.

"Oh, darlin', you shouldn't be carryin' that." Strong arms quickly grasped the tray and removed it from her hands. "Now, where do you want this?"

Bailey stared at Trevor Anderson while she swiped at her sweaty forehead. "Where did you come from, cowboy?" She pointed at the sink. "Put the dishes there, please. The dishwasher will get here and take care of them after school lets out."

Trevor gazed at her, his soft brown eyes assessing. "Well, thank heavens for that. I was kind of hoping I could escape dishpan hands." He grinned as he waved his fingers in front of her.

Bailey's gaze flew to his hands. They were clean and well-tended. Almost as if he got regular manicures. Interesting. She nodded at a vase of flowers sitting on the counter. "Who got flowers?"

Spencer blew into the room carrying a few empty trays and dumped them in the sink. He turned to Trevor and winked. "Are those for me, cowboy?"

Trevor's face reddened. "Not exactly." He plucked the card attached to the vase and handed it to Bailey.

She slit the envelope and pulled out the card. "Thank you for my tea party. I especially loved the chocolate scones. Evie." Bailey raised an eyebrow. "Your granddaughter?"

Trevor nodded.

Bailey smiled. "Well, please thank her for the flowers and the note. But she didn't have to send me flowers. I was well paid."

"I suggested the flowers. Thought a *purty* lady like you deserved them."

Bailey slowly slid down into a chair and expelled a tired sigh. "Well, thank you. That's very sweet. It's been a while since anyone sent me flowers."

Spencer huffed and muttered, "That's because there is a decided lack of gentlemen in the Greater Milwaukee area. Bunch of peasants without a clue, all of them."

Bailey shot him a tired smile. "Maybe it's because you're chasing so many of them, I don't have a chance."

Spencer preened. "Then I guess you better make your move on this cowboy before he takes a walk on the wild side."

A strange look crossed Trevor's face. He obviously didn't know how to react when a man flirted with him.

Bailey pushed herself up from her chair and made a face. "I have to get ready for afternoon tea." She gazed at Spencer. "How's the scone situation?"

"I have fully restored the coffers. Just give me a list of today's offerings and I'll start setting up the tiers."

"Watercress, egg salad, caprese, and a mini-apple and chicken panini on the sandwich tier. Lemon blueberry, raspberry white chocolate, and maple nut on the scone tier. For the dessert tier, we have chocolate pots de crème, strawberry cheesecake, lemon sunshine cake, and date-apricot-nut bars."

Spencer nodded and went into the refrigerator to begin assembly.

"Wow, you've really got your hands full. Did you bake all that?" Trevor gazed at Bailey.

Bailey shrugged. "Only some of it. I formed a baking co-op with some stay-at-home moms in the area. I pay them for weekly treats, but they also exchange with each other. Everyone benefits. I always have something new on hand. Thank God." She kneaded her neck. "I've been wrestling with some stiff increases in ingredient costs, though. I wish I could find a small farm where I can grow most of what we need here. I'm sure some moms would help, and it might be educational to get their kids involved, too." She went to the sink and washed her hands. "I had someone look at the roof, to see if I could do it up there, but they didn't think it could hold the weight." She sighed. "Plus, our growing months are seriously limited. From May to October, if we're lucky. But that's a project for another day. I have lots of dreams, but no time."

"I get it. Homegrown is always better." He took her hand and gently held it. "You're busy, so I'll be on my way. Wonderful to see you again, Bailey." He brought her hand to his lips and gently kissed her knuckles. "Until next time."

Stunned at the heat generated by his touch, Bailey blushed. "I hope there is a next time." She stumbled over her words. "I mean, I . . . "

Trevor gazed at her with heat. "Oh, there will be." He let go of her hand and strolled out the back door.

Spencer appeared at the kitchen entrance and fanned his face. "Well, butter my butt and call me a biscuit. That was *hawt*, sizzling *hawt*." He squealed. "Oh Lordy, Miss Bailey's got herself a man."

Bailey squinted at the clock on the wall as her fifth attempt at a chocolate peppermint whipped cream cake baked. Thank God Spencer had the early baking shift tomorrow. It was moving on to midnight, and she needed at least a few more hours to experiment.

Just as she was removing the cake from the oven, she heard a loud crash and the burglar alarm went off. She all but dropped the two pans onto cooling racks and raced out into the dining room.

What the ever-loving hell? Someone had broken her front window. Reaching for her bat behind the cash register, Bailey's eyes swept the room. Was she alone? Had someone gotten in? Carefully, she crept to the window and spotted two teenage boys running away. Probably best if she didn't chase them. She shivered. The hole was small, but the night air had to be below zero. She would need to patch up the window before the indoor temps dropped as well. That might mess with the water pipes.

Her foot bumped into a large stone. She stared at it for a minute, confused. Bailey was still staring at the rock when the police pulled up, their emergency lights flashing.

An officer walked toward the hole in the glass and asked, "Ma'am. Are you okay?"

Bailey shook her head. Suddenly, she felt like she was speaking through a heavy fog. "Someone broke my window." She frowned. Why had someone done that? Bailey looked up. "Why the heck would they break my window? I sell scones and finger sandwiches. I don't keep money in the register. There's nothing to take." She wrung her hands and fought back tears.

The officer shook his head. "I don't know, ma'am. Sometimes, vandals just like to stir up trouble. Can you turn off the alarm and let us in so we can get your statement?"

Bailey shook her head sharply. "Oh . . . I'm sorry, I guess

I'm just . . ." Still dazed, she slowly walked to the door and punched a code into the alarm, then unlocked the door. She pushed it open for the officers.

One officer stood in front of her and offered a slight smile. He led her to a chair and motioned her to sit. Kneeling in front of her, he gazed at Bailey. "Ma'am, you've had a big shock. Just take a few deep breaths. That's it. In and out."

Bailey stared at the officer. "Okay. I *mean* I'm okay."

The other officer rubbed his arms. "It's freezing in here already. Why don't we cover the hole up before your pipes freeze?" He gazed around the dining room and pointed at a plastic placemat sticking out from under a lace doily. "If you have tape, I can cover the hole with that. It's not a permanent solution, but it should help keep the heat in until someone boards up the window."

Bailey barely heard what the officer said. She tugged at her ponytail and released her hair. The last thing she wanted to deal with was some kid's destructive impulses. Little shits should be at home in bed. It was after midnight and tomorrow was a school day.

The officer tried again. "Ma'am, some tape?"

Bailey stared at him. Why did he want tape? She shivered again. "It's so cold. We need to board up that window."

The other officer gazed at his partner. "I'm going to look around for some tape and a coat. She seems to be in some kind of shock."

After he walked away, Bailey frowned. "The tape is in the drawer by the sink and my coat is hanging by the door," she yelled. She gazed at the officer now standing in front of her. "I'm Bailey Willis, the owner, and you are?"

"Officer Peter Benson, ma'am." He opened his notepad. He gestured toward the other officer. "He's Officer Krank. Now, I've already got your store details from the security company, so just tell me what happened. What did you hear? What did you see? Start at the beginning."

Officer Krank came back with Bailey's coat and gently placed it around her shoulders. Then he used duct tape and two plastic placemats to cover the hole in the window.

Bailey closed her eyes and tried to recall the series of events. "I was baking in the kitchen. I checked the clock. It was around midnight, so I knew I was probably going to be here a few more hours." She pursed her lips. "Wasn't happy about that. Then the timer went off, and I took a cake out of the oven. I heard a crash and glass breaking, then the alarm went off." She picked up the baseball bat at her side. "I came into the dining room, picked up my bat, and tried to figure out if anyone had broken in. It seemed safe, so I went to the hole in the window and looked out. Two kids were running down the street."

"Can you describe them?"

"Um, both skinny. One was shorter than the other and had one of those beanies on, but he had light hair." She scrunched her nose. "The streetlight was flickering again, so it was hard to see, but the other one was wearing a hoodie. A dark one, I think."

The front door suddenly opened. Spencer rushed in, wearing Batman pajamas covered by a down jacket, his spiky red hair plastered to the side of his head as if he had been sleeping. "Bailey, what the hell?" He rushed to her and started patting her arms. "Are you okay?"

Officer Krank touched Spencer's shoulder and tried to nudge him away. "Sir, this woman has just had a big shock. Give her some room."

Spencer spun around and snarled. "Unless you have permission, don't touch." He kneeled at Bailey's side and cooed, "Are you okay?"

Bailey frowned at him. "Spence, you should be in bed. Why are you even here?"

"When my scanner went off and I heard this address, I didn't think. I was not about to allow someone to trash my workplace."

"You could have just called."

Spencer glared. "Well, if someone had their phone on, that might have been a possibility." He sniffed the air. "Baking in the middle of the night alone, with only Barney Fife and friend to protect you, is just plain stupid. You could have gotten hurt." His voice rose. "Someone could have attacked or molested or shot or —"

Bailey snapped out of her fog. "Spence, focus. And don't insult members of our police force. Some vandals broke my window and ran off. What were they going to steal? Scones?"

Spencer threw up his hands. "Sometimes, there's just no reasoning with you. Put your coat on. I'm taking you home."

"Not before I board up this window." She turned to the police officers, who almost seemed amused. "Surely, there's someplace I can call in an emergency?"

The officer who was interviewing Bailey pulled out a business card and handed it to her. "This is a group of firemen and police who do repair and renovation off-duty. They're pretty good. Call the number and leave a message. Someone checks it every hour." He took out a card and wrote something on it. "You can pick up the report for your insurance company after ten tomorrow morning at the station. That's the case number. Meanwhile, get that window boarded up." They turned and left the tea shop.

"Oh, nothing like a sweaty fireman flexing all of those muscles," Spencer crowed as he bounced in his chair. "Call them. I'll wait right here with you." He sat in a chair with a big grin on his face.

Bailey stared at him. "I thought you were taking me home." She shook her head. "Not like it's far."

Someone cleared their throat and Bailey whipped around

in her chair. She grabbed at the table beside her to steady herself.

Trevor, dressed in pajama pants, a tee shirt, down jacket, and his cowboy hat, frowned. "Kid, if you wanted to keep Bailey company, why'd you call and tell me to *get my fine butt to the shop*?

Spencer's mouth dropped open. He held up his arms defensively. "When I called, I didn't know there'd be firemen. I mean, why wouldn't I miss my beauty sleep for a fireman?"

"There won't be any firemen." Trevor held up a toolbox. "You can get the plywood and saw out of the back of my truck and be on your way." He smirked. "Unless you want to watch *me* getting all hot and sweaty?"

Spencer fiercely shook his head. "No siree, I don't poach . . ." He pulled on his jacket and gave Trevor a haughty look. "Besides, you're a bit old for me."

Bailey's face flamed, and she buried her head in her hands. This night was going from bad to worse. "You didn't need to get out of bed to rescue me, Trevor. I would have figured something out."

Trevor walked over to her chair and pulled Bailey into his arms. He hugged her tightly. "Bet no one bothered to give you the hug you so sorely need."

Bailey sank into Trevor's warmth. His embrace calmed her. His heart was beating steady and strong. She closed her eyes and listened, taking comfort from that.

"I was just getting out of the shower when the kid called. My son-in-law hosted a poker game tonight. Between the cigars and cigarettes, I was feeling kind of ripe when I cashed out. You'd think medical professionals would know better than to pollute their lungs with that crap."

Bailey emitted a small sob. She couldn't hold it in anymore. Someone had attacked her baby. That hurt. Really hurt. This shop was the culmination of a drastic career change. After almost twenty years as a lawyer, she had tired of the law game and lawyers. That forced her to take a hard look at her life and find a better path. Baking was Bailey's fallback, her stress reliever. After visiting a few tearooms in the United Kingdom, Bailey fell in love with the rituals surrounding tea. And she found a reason to launch a new chapter in her life.

The vandals had done more than break a window — they had threatened her dream. She almost felt violated. *How dare they?* The tears started flowing. Angry tears. Dammit, she was so sick of all the hate generated by the pandemic, politics, and abuse of power. Sometimes, she felt like the civilized world was spinning out of control.

Trevor hugged her more tightly. "Let it out, honey. You've had a heck of a scare."

That was all it took. She sobbed uncontrollably.

Trevor ran his hands down her back, attempting to comfort her. "Have a good cry, then we'll sit down and figure out a way to stop this from happening again."

"I fought so hard to make this shop work, to make it a success." She emitted a slight hiccup. "And with a stupid rock, they crushed me. I feel like they threw me on the floor and stomped all over me,"

Trevor kissed her hair. "If it was kids, I imagine they don't understand what this shop means to you, nor do they care. Kids are impulsive. They do stupid things. Chances are they don't know you and have never been in your shop. They saw an opportunity for a little fun and they took it. That big window was irresistible to them." Bailey shivered. Trevor pulled back and wiped away her tears. "Now, let's get your coat fully on and get you off your feet. I'll make you a cup of tea and then board up your window. After that, I'll take you home."

Bailey nodded. She struggled to find the sleeves for her coat and finally pulled it on.

Trevor smiled at her sweetly and pulled up the zipper. He

felt around for her pockets and pulled out a pair of mittens decorated with rolling pins. He smirked but said nothing. Instead, he pulled them over Bailey's hands. "Okay, let's sit you down and I'll go make you tea."

He gently guided her to a chair, but Bailey stopped him. She shook her head. "No, don't leave me alone. I don't want to be alone."

"Okay, then." He grabbed her hand and led her to the kitchen, then sat her at a table and rummaged around for tea.

Bailey watched mutely as he heated water in the microwave and dropped a tea bag into a mug. He went into the cooler and came back with sugar cubes, cream, and a scone. He made a face. "I wasn't sure what was the best way to get some sugar in you." He put everything on a tray and led Bailey back into the dining room. Gently, he pushed her into a chair and served her the tea.

Who is this man? Bailey was used to being the person doling out kindness. She wasn't used to receiving it. She attempted to smile at Trevor. "Thank you for taking care of me." She lifted the teacup to her mouth and groaned with pleasure. "Nothing better than chamomile after a stressful situation."

Trevor nodded in acknowledgment, then went to work. He quickly cut out two boards and somehow attached one to each side of the window. When he was done, the tea shop warmed up. "That should hold you until you get the glass replaced. Maybe you should also upgrade to something that someone can't break into." He packed away his tools and cleaned up the area. He smiled at Bailey. "Now that your shop is secure, it's time to get you home."

Bailey giggled.

Trevor lifted an eyebrow. "Why is that funny?"

"I live upstairs. It's a short commute."

"Well then, let's lock up and put you to bed."

Bailey blushed. "No need, I can lock up and head upstairs

by myself."

Trevor gently lifted her hand and kissed her palm. "I insist. You've had a rough night." He glanced at the clock on the wall. "Or rather, morning. Let's get you tucked in. I imagine you need some sleep before your shop opens."

Bailey yawned. "If I can sleep. I'm so tired, but I doubt I can get my brain to shut off. Thankfully, Spence opens tomorrow. I'm going to have to deal with the police and the insurance company, then get that window fixed."

"Even more reason to get you to bed." Trevor turned off the main lights and slid his arm around Bailey. "Come on, let's get you upstairs. The sun will be up soon enough." Gently, he pushed her forward. "Lead the way."

Chapter Three: Bourbon Makes Everything Better

When Bailey finally rose, it was way past her traditional waking hour.

She stretched her arms and groaned. Last night had been a beast, a shock to her system. She was not looking forward to dealing with the police or her insurance company today. "Assholes will probably raise my premiums." Bailey rolled over in bed and planted her feet on the floor. She hurried through a shower, dried her hair, and dressed in jeans and an old band tee. She would put on the chef's coat later.

After locking her apartment, she grabbed her purse and coat and slowly descended into the tea shop kitchen.

Spencer looked up from the mixer he was running and smiled. "Finally, the lady awakes. How are you feeling?"

"Ugh. I'm dreading all the red tape this morning. I have to go to the police station, contact the insurance company, then call to get the window fixed. Such a pain."

Spencer frowned. "Why? The window's fixed. And it's that triple-paned stuff. You know, the kind that can take a bullet? Come take a look." He turned off the mixer, wiped his hands on a towel, and led her through the swinging kitchen doors.

Puzzled, Bailey followed. She gazed at the large picture window. It *was* no longer boarded up. She moved closer. A triple-paned window, something she had avoided because of the expense. Someone had even taken the time to wipe the window down. There wasn't a single fingerprint to be had.

"What the heck?" She turned to Spencer. "Did they leave an invoice? Or warranty information?"

Spencer shrugged. "I got here at six and saw the new window already installed." He grinned. "Think about it. Who had the knowledge and the means to get that window fixed so quickly?"

Bailey shook her head. "Trevor?"

Spencer giggled. "Me thinks the boss has a serious suitor." He turned toward the kitchen, humming a jaunty tune about getting married in the morning.

Bailey stared at him. "Why on earth would Trevor replace my window? We aren't even dating or anything."

He pointed behind her. "Yet."

Bailey gazed over her shoulder. Trevor stood there holding a huge bouquet of flowers. He strolled toward her and placed them in her arms. "I was hoping I'd get back before you woke up. I thought this might help get your day off to a better start."

Bailey smiled at him. She sniffed the flowers, then stood on her toes to kiss his cheek. "You didn't think the new window was enough"

Trevor blushed. "Just trying to give you a helping hand."

Bailey cocked an eyebrow. "You woke someone up at three in the morning to install a new window? That must have cost a fortune." She tilted her head. "Did you even get any sleep?"

Trevor shrugged. "Enough. My son-in-law knew a guy, and he came out in the middle of the night, so I took advantage of that. Why not? You've got that lovely smile back on your face. That's all that matters. Unfortunately, all he had in stock was a triple-pane security window, so I took it."

"I have insurance, you know. Do you have a receipt so I can get you reimbursed?"

"Nope."

"Come on, let me at least pay you back."

"Nope. No need."

Bailey stared at him. "Well, if you won't take money, can I at least take you to dinner? We have some great steakhouses here. I'm sure you'd love them."

Trevor chuckled. "I think I'm being stereotyped. Just because I raise Longhorns does not mean I eat them. I'd much prefer something a little lighter, like pasta or Chinese."

Bailey's face reddened. "I didn't mean to . . . oh, darn it, I guess I did. But we've got Mexican, Thai, Chinese, Italian, Japanese, Polish, Middle Eastern, and German around here and most other types of food. Take your pick."

"I've got a better idea. How about I cook for you?"

Bailey frowned. "How does that pay you back for helping me?"

"All I want in return is the pleasure of your company, darlin'. You and me in front of a fire, eatin' a delicious meal with great wine and, of course, a divine dessert. That's all I need."

"Will you at least let me cook for you?"

"I'll let you help. But in the kitchen, I have one rule. I'm in charge."

Bailey huffed. *We'll see about that.*

This woman.

Trevor didn't understand his attraction. She was a force. Not that many people would ditch years of education and an established professional career and start over. It was intriguing. He knew way too many people who claimed to hate their jobs, their lives, and even their spouses, but woke up every day and did it all over again. Not his Bailey. She took the bull by the horns and changed her path. She built a new business from the ground up. She was a warrior princess in every sense of the word. He respected the hell out of that.

Some men might find her single-mindedness off-putting, even emasculating. Yet, he found it invigorating. She made him want more.

Despite her ferocity, last night he had witnessed her softer side. It shook her up that the vandals broke her window, and she wasn't embarrassed to admit it. She'd needed comfort and a sense of security, and she hadn't been afraid to reach for it. Correction, reach for him.

It sorely tempted him when he tucked Bailey into bed. He had to hold himself back from crawling in beside her. He'd wanted to hold her, feel her softness and her womanly curves, kiss every inch of her, and assure her he'd keep her safe. But that wasn't his place. The Texas gentleman in him knew it was just too soon.

Instead, he'd woken up his son-in-law Billy and asked for a recommendation for an emergency window repair. Trevor offered the guy a bonus to come out and replace the window before morning. There was no way he was going to allow the vandals to disrupt Bailey's business. Nor did he want her reminded of that traumatic event. He'd wanted her to wake with a clean slate.

Trevor was not sure where the sudden need to protect Bailey had come from. Maybe it was because last night he had seen through her *tough guy* façade. He didn't know why Spencer had alerted him to the vandalism at the shop, but he was thankful. The kid was mostly a pain in the ass, but he was loyal to Bailey and had proved it with a simple phone call.

"She's gonna need you tonight, cowboy," Spencer had said. "Someone attacked her shop. The cops are on the way. But I know Bailey, and she's going to take that broken window personally. It will shake her up, but it would be weird for me to comfort her. I can only do so much. She needs someone more seasoned. I choose you. Besides, you're from Texas and you're a cowboy. It's a matter of honor."

"Kid, we barely know each other. Why would she want me there?"

Spencer had sighed dramatically. "Here's your chance to

make your move. I've seen the way you look at her, and she practically swoons whenever you're near her. I'm telling you that this is your chance. Take it or mess it up. It's up to you."

"How'd you get my number, anyway?"

"Your daughter put it on the order slip. I might have entered it into the system. Just in case." He paused. "Now get your fine ass to the shop."

Trevor had harrumphed. The kid was sneaky. But his affection for Bailey proved him to be solid.

Once Trevor knew Bailey was in need, he all but ran to the shop and took over. Not because he believed Bailey needed him, but because she didn't deserve to have to deal with that mess on her own.

And now he had a date with Bailey. It bugged the hell out of him that he owed Spencer for that, but he'd find a way to thank him. Maybe he could find the kid his own cowboy. Or maybe a Yankee who wore cowboy hats.

Bailey didn't know what to think when she turned into the driveway at the address Trevor specified.

The home was large and obviously expensive. It was in one of those fancy neighborhoods in Franklin, where some homes had Olympic-size pools in their basements. It also had a *for sale* sign leaning against the garage. Was Trevor buying or selling this place? Bailey shrugged. Just another mystery that was Trevor Anderson. She knew he was intelligent and kind. He seemed filled with good humor and just a touch of arrogance. He knew how to take charge in an emergency. He had a smile that lit up her heart and a face that made her girly parts melt. How long had it been since anyone had made her feel that way?

Just as she was turning off her car, the front door flew open and Trevor waved, wearing an apron that proclaimed *Kiss the cook and you might get dinner.* Bailey chuckled. She wouldn't mind testing that one out. In fact . . . Bailey stepped out of her car and marched right up to Trevor, a sly expression on her face. Before Trevor could greet her, she pulled his lips to hers and kissed him thoroughly. She wasn't polite about it, nor was she restrained.

At first, Trevor hesitated, then he pulled her closer and unleashed his tongue, joining hers in a heated dance. He chuckled. "Darlin', why the hell are we making out in this cockshrinking cold when we could be inside before a roaring fire?"

Bailey smirked. "I just wanted to make sure I got dinner." She pointed to his apron.

Trevor grinned. "Well, how about we continue this in a more pleasurable setting?" He led her into the expensive home and closed the door. He took her coat and tossed it onto a banister.

Bailey eyes rounded. The interior of the house was decorated as if Christmas had exploded. There were two glittery trees in the living room, and pine boughs with ribbons, and multi-colored lights everywhere. There were also large statues of nutcrackers lined up against one wall and an elegantly carved Santa posted at the fireplace. She saw statues of angels of all shapes and sizes scattered throughout, even on the stairs.

Bailey couldn't hide her smirk. "This is not how I expected a cowboy to decorate for Christmas. Maybe you should move some of this outside. Your front yard looks like the Grinch lives here."

Trevor chuckled. "Believe me, I had nothing to do with this. This is all Bevvy. She said it adds pizazz. I think she intended to have some sort of party here until I moved in." Trevor blinked. "All this makes my eyes hurt. I just wanted to give you the Bevvy experience." He hit a switch and all the lights went off.

"Much better." Bailey sniffed the air. "What are you making? It smells heavenly."

"Coq Au Vin."

Bailey stared at him. "Where on earth did you learn how to make Coq Au Vin?"

Trevor shrugged. "After my wife died, I spent some time in Paris. It was her favorite place. We traveled there at least once a year." He ran a hand through his thick, dark hair. "I was pretty lost. One minute, we were arguing about Bevvy's choice of school—she wanted to go to some fancy boarding school in Switzerland. The next, the sheriff is at my door telling me a semi plowed into my wife's car and killed her." His voice grew soft, the memory still painful. "I was pretty lost. For years. Finally, my sons bought me a ticket to Paris and told me to work through my grief and get my act together, though they didn't use those exact words."

He half-smiled. "So I went. For the first few weeks, I just wandered around, visiting the places we had enjoyed together. Then I got bored, but I wasn't ready to leave. My wife and I had always talked about taking a French cooking class. So, I asked around, found one, and attended for the both of us. When I finished, I felt like I had a new purpose. I kept attending classes until I was ready to go home." He smiled. "Cooking got me through some rough times, and now I cook to relax."

Bailey smiled. "When were you in Paris?"

"Five years ago."

"Me, too. I did a stint at Le Cordon Bleu. I came back two years ago. In fact . . ." She walked to Trevor and removed his hat. She studied his face. "I think I met you once. Did you take a class on bread-making? There was an American there. Slightly older, handsome, but quiet. We figured out that he was running from the law and hiding out in culinary school.

He would never join us at the clubs. Never even spoke to us. Was that you?"

Trevor shrugged. "Maybe. I was more focused on working through Mariah's death. I had no interest in socializing."

"I remember. You always seemed so sad." Bailey reached for Trevor and kissed him gently. "When that class was over, you just disappeared."

"One day, I woke up and was just ready to go home. So, I did." He pulled Bailey closer and trailed kisses down her neck. His hands ran down her back, and she shivered. "I don't remember you, though I was kind of out of it." He cocked his head. "How about you? You're a beautiful woman. Confident, smart, successful. Never married? No interest in a relationship?"

Bailey shrugged, and a sad expression crossed her face. "I met the man I thought was the love of my life in my thirties. We had a wild, passionate affair. Before I knew it, we were engaged. I was ready to get married right away. I was all in. He kept delaying. By accident, I found out he wasn't as single as he claimed — separated but undecided about divorce. I was the backup plan.".

She attempted a smile. "It crushed me. It was a long time before I trusted again. I've dated, but . . ." She sighed. "How can I say this? In my thirties, I was in a rush to get married and have kids. Now, I'm not sure marriage is even necessary."

"I guess it all depends on who you meet and whether you want them in your life, permanently." A timer rang. Trevor grabbed her hand. "Let's eat, then we can sit in front of the fire and talk some more."

Bailey groaned and pushed back from the dining table. "Oh, my Lord, that was decadent. Julia Child's recipe, but with a few tweaks. The parsnips and that white Burgundy really took it to the next level." She hugged her midsection. "My stomach is doing a happy dance."

Trevor grinned. "It's a big hit with the cowhands on my ranch, too."

Bailey's mouth dropped open. "You serve Coq Au Vin to your ranch employees?"

Trevor stood and began clearing the table. "Why not? They have to eat, too. Besides, they do most of their own cooking in the bunkhouse. When I cook, they expect something special. And they get it. Some of those men have been with me for over forty years. We've been through everything together. Marriages. Divorces, Births. Deaths. And all the drama in between." He removed the last dish from the table. "Wait until you taste my dessert." He left the room and returned with what looked like brownies. "Now these have made grown men cry."

Bailey made a face. "Brownies? That hardly seems like a culinary challenge." She lifted one off the platter and took a bite. Her eyes widened, and she took another bite. She tasted caramel, chocolate, nuts, and something else. She couldn't put her finger on it. She stared at the brownie and scrunched her nose. "What is this? It's divine."

Trevor preened in a very manly way. "My bourbon caramel truffle brownies." He grinned. "Do you like them?"

Bailey's mouth was full, so she just nodded.

"I thought they warranted a Texas twist, thus the bourbon. As you know, bourbon makes almost anything better."

"These are amazing. I would love to serve these at the tea shop."

Trevor's eyes narrowed. He growled, "Are you trying to poach my brownies?"

Bailey giggled. "No, I'd include you in my Baker's Coop. You bake them, I pay for them."

An evil grin formed on his lips. "And I know just how I want you to pay for them."

Bailey studied him, her expression sly. "I think that's illegal, at least around here."

"Not if you're dating the boss." Trevor waited until Bailey finished her brownie, then he gently nudged her out of her chair. "Let's relax in front of the fire. My daughter's allowing me to stay here for a few more weeks, but after the first of the year, she's selling it. It's her hobby. She flips houses for pocket money, as she says. Anyhow, might as well take advantage while we can." He drew her down onto a thick fluffy rug and laid her underneath him.

Suddenly, his lips seemed to be everywhere, setting off flares of heat as he explored Bailey's body. She was barely conscious of him removing her clothes. Her body was on fire and she yearned for more. She caressed his head, running her hands through his hair. She wanted him to devour her. Bailey was long past the slut-shaming that often accompanied one-night stands. She was old enough to appreciate opportunities when they arose. And at her age, that wasn't often. Besides, this was a first date, not necessarily only one night. She intended to enjoy this man for as long as he was interested.

Trevor's lips went to her breasts, and Bailey shuddered. He licked, then sucked her nipples into fine points. His hand joined his lips, and he tugged hard. "Darlin', these nipples are lethal. They're just beggin' for clamps."

Clamps? Bailey wanted to purr. She really loved a man who was adventurous in the bedroom. Trevor bit down hard on her nipple and Bailey's body bucked against him. The pain ripped through her, then settled into a disturbingly pleasant haze. Trevor bit down on the other nipple and Bailey merely whimpered. She was feeling scattered and overheated. She didn't want it to end.

Trevor's hand brushed her stomach and trailed a finger down into her pussy. He stroked her lips, then tugged at her clit. His lips left her breasts and followed his fingers. He nudged her legs farther apart and lapped at her core. "Mmmm." His tongue darted in and out of her cunt, aggressively sucking and licking.

Heat blossomed in her core, and Bailey's mind threatened to unravel. Trevor inserted two fingers inside her, and Bailey screamed. She began thrashing all over, her mind reaching for the climax that hovered just out of reach. Bailey tried to ride Trevor's hand, seeking some kind of relief. Two fingers became three and Bailey thrust down harder. "Please, Trevor. More. Harder. Don't stop."

Trevor increased the pressure, roughly driving his fingers in and out of her cunt. He sucked on her clit hard, then bit down. He murmured, "Come for me, darlin'."

Bailey's body arched, and she roared. Her mind blanked, then exploded into a wondrous kaleidoscope of colors. Her body twisted and shuddered violently. As her climax slowly dissipated, Bailey realized Trevor was embracing her, his strong arms protective as she settled into total bliss. She burrowed against his chest, and a mewl of contentment escaped her lips as she drifted . . .

The scent of chocolate roused Bailey. She sniffed and leisurely opened her eyes.

Trevor had wrapped her in a very soft blanket and placed a pillow under her head. She felt content. "What is that smell?" She sat up and pulled the blanket around her shoulders.

"Chocolat Chaud, Texas style. As you probably remember, in France, they make hot chocolate with melted chocolate and milk. It is rich and decadent. Nothing like the heavily diluted powdered version Americans drink."

Trevor leaned down from his armchair, picked Bailey up as if she weighed nothing, and settled her on his lap. She cuddled into him and closed her eyes. When something nudged her lips, she opened them. Trevor held a steaming mug. "Take a sip."

Bailey drank a small amount and moaned. "Oh, that's heavenly." She took another sip. The drink was a rich milk chocolate with a hint of mint. The right amount of mint. The amount she was seeking for her cake. She gazed at Trevor. "What did you use to make this? How did you get that quality of mint?"

Trevor removed the mug from her hands and drank. He frowned. "I don't know. I just used a box of chocolates Bevvy gave me. She gives them out at Christmas time. Says they're the best chocolates around." He grunted. "Maybe in the Northlands . . . "

Bailey sat up, ignoring the blanket that fell to the floor. "Show me."

She tried to stand, but Trevor restrained her. "Please tell me what was shapin' up to be a very romantic evening will not be ruined with a recipe chat."

Bailey turned and gazed at him. Dammit, Trevor looked hurt. Hurt like a little boy who had his truck stolen *hurt*. Even she wasn't that cold. "Promise me you'll hang onto that box." She settled back against him and nuzzled his neck. "Now, you'd better turn up the heat, cowboy. I'm getting a little chilly."

CHAPTER FOUR: WHERE ART THOU PEPPERMINT?

Trevor sat on a stool in Bailey's kitchen as she melted a box of the chocolate mints he'd provided.

"You know," he drawled. "This would be much more entertaining if all you were wearing was that apron. As thanks for possibly solving your cake dilemma."

Bailey ignored him. "Shush. I'm trying to focus on the recipe. When the cake's in the oven, you'll get your reward."

Trevor's eyebrows shot up, but he remained silent. He was a patient man. Mostly. But the memory of the delectable Bailey in his bed . . . well, his stiff cock hadn't taken a breather since that night. Some of his friends complained about ED and the four-hour hard-ons from their shots or pills, but he didn't need any medical assistance. Apparently, little Bailey Willis was all he needed to perform.

He couldn't believe that this woman had once toiled as a lawyer. She wasn't stuffy or obsessed with work. Instead, she was a lovely, sophisticated woman with a giggle that stirred his soul and a smile that stirred his cock. With her wavy blonde hair and luminous blue eyes, she was a feast for the eyes and a treat for the loins. When it was time for him to return to Texas, it was going to physically hurt to leave her behind. Even watching her cook was a delight. *Lordy Trevor, you've got it bad.*

Bailey finished mixing all the ingredients and filled two round cake pans. She slid them into the oven, efficiently rinsed her baking tools and bowls, and wiped off the counter. With a grin, she turned to Trevor. "Okay, we have thirty-five minutes." Bailey arced an eyebrow. "In for a little bronco-riding?"

Laughing, Trevor crooked a finger. "Your metaphor needs work, but I'm going to assume you'll be doing the riding?"

Bailey sauntered over and ran a finger down his chest. "With pleasure," she cooed. She nipped at his lips, grabbed his hand, and pulled him off the stool. She led Trevor to her large leather couch. Hastily, she tugged off his clothes. "Thank God, you don't have those boots on."

Trevor yanked at her apron and the clothing beneath. He tossed her jeans, shirt, and underwear across the room. "You won't be needing these tonight."

Bailey pushed Trevor onto the sofa and grabbed his cowboy hat off a nearby side table. She pulled it onto her head and climbed on top of him. With a sly grin, she grabbed his rigid cock and slid it inside of her. With a whoop, she swung her arm over her head and rode Trevor like a prize bull. She bounced up and down on his cock, then circled her hips — giggling, mewling, and moaning. With another whoop, she slammed her pussy down — again and again.

Trevor's eyes grew wide as he gazed at Bailey. She was wild. He reached for her bouncing breasts, but Bailey pushed him away, wagging her finger. Then she bucked against him, driving his cock deeper within her. Trevor tried to say something, but she pinned his lips shut with a finger and shook her head. This was going to be a one-woman show. While Trevor wasn't averse to being treated like a stallion, a stud horse, he'd never had a woman take charge like this before. It was disconcerting. Not unenjoyable, just disconcerting. Hell, his cock was getting a workout, and it certainly wasn't objecting to the ride. And Bailey was a vision. Her face flushed, her hair was flying, and her body was . . .

Bailey threw back her head and screamed. She shuddered and spasmed, then slammed down on Trevor's cock one last time. He groaned loudly as her pussy squeezed his cock and brought him to the brink. Bailey collapsed on top of him, his fully engorged cock still inside her.

Trevor held her tightly as he pumped and thrust a few more times. His balls tightened, and finally, he exploded. He held her tight as he rode out his orgasm. "Damn, woman. That was one hell of a ride."

The timer for the oven went off and Bailey groaned. Slowly, she slid off Trevor and stumbled to the oven. Unaware that she was leaving little puddles of cum on the floor, she grabbed a toothpick, opened the oven door, and stuck it into each cake. "Okay, you're done." She removed the pans, set them on a cooling rack, and reset the timer. She grinned sleepily at Trevor and cocked her head. "I have fifteen minutes, Any thoughts?"

Trevor sat up and beckoned. "I'm sure I can think of something. Come back here, darling, and set for a spell." He patted his lap and arched an eyebrow. "Daddy'll tell you a bedtime tale."

Bailey laughed and rolled her eyes. "I've already got a daddy, and bedtime tales are overrated." She climbed into his lap, facing him. "But you have other talents." She ran a hand across his hairy chest and cooed. "I love it when you're naked." She kissed him, and her tongue caressed his. One hand went around his head as she pulled him closer, and with the other, she tweaked a nipple. Against his mouth, she whispered, "I would love to use those clamps you bought me on you."

Trevor moaned. God, this woman was bold. He was used to simpering and well-lacquered socialites who attempted to seduce him with surgically altered bodies, willing smiles, and come-hither eyes—usually framed with unnatural false eyelashes. There was nothing fake about Bailey. She was a real woman. Hell, unlike the women who pursued him in the Lone Star state, she didn't even try to hide the gray hair making subtle appearances in her luscious mane. Bailey knew who and what she was, and she was proud of it. Dammit, he was falling. But he was also leaving. What the hell was he supposed to do about that?

He nuzzled her neck. "Darling, stop squirming or I'm going to have to tie you down."

Bailey bit his neck, then chuckled. "Like I'd mind."

"Okay, guys. This is it." Bailey pointed at the most beautiful cake she had ever made.

The cake was a vision. It was four layers tall, filled with alternate layers of mint chocolate mousse and whipped cream. Bailey adorned the cake with whipped cream frosting and a dusting of crushed candy canes to produce a magnificent holiday dessert. Adding to the overall festive feel, she also fashioned a chain of Christmas lights using mint leaves dipped in melted milk chocolate. Each light was then sprayed with a traditional holiday color before being placed around the cake's top and bottom. All edible.

Bailey sighed. "I hope it's enough. I'm out of ideas."

Trevor grinned. "Darlin', it's perfect. Now stop stalling. Let's see what your customers say."

Her second-in-command Spencer whined. "Forget the customers. I want a bite."

Jilly slapped his stomach with her server's towel. "This isn't about you and your stomach. It's about Bailey staking a claim to fame. Something she can use to promote the shop."

Spencer huffed. "Don't forget the chance to get on the menu at the local country club. Serving it there will bring in a ton of customers."

Trevor made a face. "My daughter's a member. She's taken me there several times. The food is decent, could be better. Lots of people with money trying to impress each other. We'll need to make damn sure they don't get exclusive rights to your cake. You're going to want to serve it here and sell it on the side."

Bailey shrugged. "Not a concern. Once a lawyer, always a lawyer, with or without a shingle." She sighed deeply. "Well, let's get on with it." Using a long, serrated knife, Bailey cut horizontal slices about a half inch thick, then cut that slice into four portions. While she sliced the cake, Spencer and Jilly transferred the pieces to plates. When Bailey got through half the cake, she stopped and handed her assistants a fork. "Okay, we get the first bite, then the rest goes out to the customers in the dining room until it lasts."

Spencer took a bite. His eyebrows shot to his forehead. He took another bite and another. When he finished, he grinned. "This is amazing."

Jilly took a bite and merely nodded.

"But is it enough to win?" Bailey forked a piece into her mouth. She chewed slowly, then screwed up her face. "It's good, but I don't know if it's enough." She pointed at Trevor. "What do *you* think?"

Trevor looked down at his empty plate and his lips slowly turned up into a smile. He smacked his lips. "Besides you, it's the best thing to pass through these lips in a while."

Bailey's face reddened, and she coughed.

Spencer slapped Trevor on the arm. "Dude, that was rude, and also TMI—way too much information." Spencer glared at him. "Is that what happens when you spend too much time among copulating cows? Did you forget the rules of civility among humans?" He shuddered. "Now I've got pictures in my head that I . . ." He grabbed a couple of plates and pushed through the kitchen doors. He muttered, "Damn cowboy."

Jilly's gaze moved between Bailey and Trevor, and she sighed. "You guys are my parents' age. I know they're still doing it, and obviously, you are, too." She set her empty plate in the sink and grabbed four cake plates. "But I don't need to know about it. That's just gross." She sashayed out of the kitchen, clucking her tongue along the way.

Trevor smiled at Bailey sheepishly. "Well, damn. I feel like I've been taken out to the woodshed and spanked."

Bailey glared at him. "Well, that was kind of rude. Cute, but rude. Next time, whisper it into my ear."

Trevor pulled Bailey to him and kissed her. "Sorry, it just slipped out." He tucked a lock of hair behind her ear. "But it was the truth. That cake is the best thing I've ever tasted except for you. And I'll tell anyone who asks."

Bailey snorted. "You're a little biased. Let's see what the customers say. They're the ones that matter."

"Are you saying my opinion *doesn't* matter?" Trevor shot her a playful glare. "I think I'm insulted."

Spencer breezed back into the kitchen, holding a hand over his eyes. "Is it safe or am I going to be exposed to things I can't unsee?"

Trevor growled. "Watch it, kid. I've got almost a foot and about a hundred pounds on you."

Spencer hissed. "I know, I know. Doesn't mean you're allowed to poison the younger generation with pornographic images."

Bailey laughed. "Spence, chill. Trevor was trying to be funny. The younger generation needs to get a sense of humor. You are way too serious about life. Loosen up. Have some fun." She handed him more cake plates. "Remember to collect the customer's reactions after they try the cake. Give them that short survey I prepared." She gently pushed him back out the kitchen doors.

Bailey leaned against the counter and waited. No one else

seemed as concerned about customer reactions to her cake. The contest was only a week away. She needed her version of the chocolate peppermint whipped cream cake to be perfect. She also needed to start generating some buzz. Her little tea shop needed all the publicity it could get.

Trevor wrapped his arms around her and nuzzled her neck. "Stop worrying. Your cake is going to be a big hit and you know it."

Bailey tried not to sigh. "I really need to win this contest. I need the publicity." She made a face. "With the economy so screwed up and prices on the rise, I need to increase cash flow. If I can sell this cake as a luxury item, it will give me the financial boost I need."

Trevor frowned. "Just how tight are things?"

"Tight enough, but that's not the real problem. I need capital to expand." Bailey pursed her lips. "I had so many dreams when I went to culinary school. Unfortunately, I need cash to pursue them."

"Like what?"

"Well, a hobby farm for one. A place where I can raise everything I need for the tea shop. The fruits, berries, herbs, fresh eggs from chickens, things like that. There's still a lot of farmlands around here. Eventually, I could make it a destination — not only a tea shop, but maybe a baking school primarily for kids. I love working with kids. They're so eager to learn new things. They don't teach baking or cooking in schools anymore. Unless a grandparent or parent teaches them, how will they learn to cook for themselves? I'd love to fill that gap. And plant science is important, too. Kids need to learn where their food comes from and how to grow it if need be.

Bailey smiled. "When I was growing up, my grandparents had a farm. I loved how they lived off the land. My grandmother would go out to the garden and the barnyard to collect what she needed for their meals. Eggs from the chickens, milk from the cows and goats. Herbs for seasoning. What she didn't share with others, she dried or canned. It was such a simple way to live."

Trevor caressed her hand. "There are lots of things you could grow to make your own tea and desserts."

"I know. And when the ingredients are fresh, everything will taste better, brighter."

"About the only thing you couldn't grow is the cacao."

Bailey held up a finger. "Not outdoors, but what if you could create the proper growing environment indoors? With humidity and temperature control, I think it's possible. I only need a few bushes, so it wouldn't take much, just attention to detail."

"Might be easier just to import the beans. Even the nibs."

"I know, but few can claim they grew their own." Bailey shrugged. "At the very least, I can contract with a grower in the US. But I like the idea of being self-sustaining for everything. I've got a brother who can build anything. He can take an idea and create what's needed. It's amazing how his mind works, and the best thing is, he has a real sweet tooth. He'll work for desserts." She paused, now lost in her dream. "Think about what a teaching tool that could be for kids. From farm to table. The wave of the future. Especially with climate change. As things heat up, we're going to have to grow things differently. Away from the droughts and excessively hot sun."

Trevor studied her. "That's going to be a lot of work, and require a lot of help, but it's doable. Heck, I found the ingredients for those mint chocolates online. With a little experimenting, you could create your own."

Bailey nodded. "I'm going to need my own cowboys to run most things." She winked at Trevor. "Too bad you're leaving after the holidays. You'd make a great partner."

Trevor nodded. "And I have a million ideas about how you

could pull it off."

Spencer waltzed back into the kitchen, carrying an empty tray. "Gawd, those people are animals. I can't believe they had the nerve to ask for more. One woman wanted me to wrap up a piece for her husband." He sniffed. "I have it on good authority that she doesn't have a husband. What a glutton."

Bailey suppressed a giggle. It was unprofessional to laugh at customers, but some of them slipped anything and everything into their purses. She routinely wrapped up anything left on the tiers after tea, but some also took the sugar cubes, tea bags, and clotted cream off the tea cart, too. One woman stuffed a China cake plate, teacup, and saucer into her purse. Much to her dismay, Bailey charged her for it. Fortunately, Bailey had heard about client pilfering. It happened at all food establishments. People helped themselves to beer pitchers and glassware at taverns. They also took bread baskets, butter trays, silverware, and wine glasses at restaurants. She expected a certain amount of theft, but it was important to watch customers, all of them.

Trevor grunted. "Why didn't you give her more?"

Spencer made a face. "That woman is always tearing Bailey down. Claims she is a better baker, better businesswoman, better everything. I wouldn't put it past her to copy the boss' recipe. I'm not about to enable her."

Bailey walked to the split doors and peered into the dining room. "Red suit, Hillary haircut?"

Spencer nodded. "Except no one that uptight could be a Democrat. She has to be a Republican."

Bailey giggled. "You'd be surprised. Politics has little influence on personality, and having no personality is not an indicator of your politics. One of the sexiest men I've ever met subscribed to politics I abhorred. There's just no predicting who drinks the Kool-Aid and who doesn't." She arched an eyebrow. "But if she's trying to steal my recipe, consider it a compliment. There's no way she'll figure it out." She winked at Trevor. "In fact, I'd welcome the challenge."

Trevor ran a hand down Bailey's back and kissed her cheek. "She's got a winner there for sure. Unbeatable."

Jilly sailed into the kitchen with her empty tray. "Lordy, those people are a little too excited about free cake." She shoved the tray into the sink. "On the plus side, they loved it. Almost everyone wanted to order the whole cake. So, once you offer it for sale, it's going to go fast." She reached into her apron pocket and pulled out a pile of surveys. "I told them if they wanted more, they had to fill out the survey."

"Oh, no, do they think they're getting more today?"

Jilly laughed. "I told them they'd have to wait until you make another one." She smirked. "You wanted buzz, I got you buzz."

Bailey grinned. "Wonderful. I want to create something that defines this place. When the old Watt's Tea Room was open in downtown Milwaukee, people went there for the Sunshine Cake, Hot Russians, and these incredible salads. I need something similar, something people will come to Hales Corners to sample. I have some ideas for other seasonal versions." She gazed at Trevor. "Like maybe a bourbon caramel whipped cream cake or a Lavender Macha whipped cream cake. There're so many ingredients to play with. And whipped cream is the perfect way to add an extra touch of class."

"Sounds delicious." Trevor wrapped his arms around Bailey, her back to his front, and rested his chin on her shoulder. He whispered into her ear, "Just like the chef."

Chapter Five: The Showstopper

Bailey rolled out of her bed and stared at the still-sleeping Trevor.

There were no two ways about it. The guy was a sprawler. He slept on his stomach, his arms and legs outstretched. If she didn't have a king-size bed, she'd have wound up on the floor. Still, she certainly wouldn't complain about sharing her bed with him. He was an all-around perfect partner. It was too bad he was going back to Texas in a few weeks. Would he stay if she asked him to? He had a whole other life there. She wasn't sure if what they had was enough—at least enough to give up his life in Texas and move permanently to Wisconsin.

Bailey picked up her phone and checked the time. As much as she wanted to take advantage of Trevor, she had to bake. Before leaving her bed, Bailey snapped a photo of his naked body. A memory she didn't want to lose when he was gone.

She quickly showered and headed down to the shop. While Jilly and Spencer handled the dining room, Bailey worked on her contest entry. It was due in the Hales Corners Village Hall at six that evening.

Bailey assembled the ingredients and placed the cakes in the oven. She whipped up the cream and set it in the refrigerator, then prepared the items she planned to use for garnish. By the time Spencer arrived, the cakes were on the cooling rack.

"Smells great in here." Spencer dramatically sniffed the air. "I'm glad we're not open yet. I don't need the customers begging for more cake. Maybe the smell of my triple chocolate scones will confuse them."

"Actually, I was thinking about those scones. What if we changed them up a bit? Instead of semisweet chocolate chips, why not use some of those in the baker's catalog? They have so many variations — mint, peanut butter, cherry, coffee, cinnamon, raspberry, and coconut. The more variety we offer, the easier it is to get customers to experiment." Bailey paused, waiting for Spencer to react. He'd either love the idea or explode at the inconvenience of change. It was more or less the toss of a coin with him.

"And here I was going to suggest we replace the nuts with freeze-dried bugs. They offer crickets, honeybees, and grasshoppers in that catalog. That will appeal to the vegan crowd."

Bailey's mouth dropped open. "Um, I'm not sure bug scones will be a hit at tea."

Spencer burst out laughing. "Oh, come on. We could call it a Honeybee Tea, with honey cake, roasted bee scones, or some sort of floral tea with different honeys. We could even serve chocolate-covered honeybees or sugar-roasted bees." He giggled. "I would love to do a blind taste-testing with some of those uppity women who prance in here."

Bailey tried to frown, but she couldn't contain her mirth. "As long as you're willing to find us fresh bees and roast them, I say go for it." She grinned. "You'd look good with one of those beekeeper hoods."

"Except I'm allergic to bee stings." He snickered. "I swell up and everything. But I'm sure Jilly would do it . . . "

Jilly slammed through the divided doors and thrust her hands on her hips. "What is it now, Spence?" She glared at him. "Another idea to make my job harder?" She shook a finger at him. "First you set me up with a total turkey, then you decide I should dress like a maid with a pink apron, no less, and now what? You want me to go bee-hunting?"

Spencer paled. "You thought Tom was a turkey? But he's

so handsome and such a gentleman . . . "

Jilly chuffed. "With nothing between the ears. My God, a woman likes to have an intelligent conversation occasionally. All he could talk about were comic books and superheroes. Does he even have a job? He paid for dinner with a bunch of ones, like he had to raid his Batman Bank to come up with the money." She made an ugly face. "And then the asshole had the nerve to imply that I owed him sex because he bought me dinner. At an Applebee's, no less. I'll bet he has a micro-penis to boot."

Spencer shook his head, flustered. "I had it on good authority that he . . . "

Bailey cleared her throat. "Boys and girls, let's not fight. I have a cake to decorate, and you have to open the shop in an hour. Let's get busy." She carefully removed the cakes from their pans and then set them back onto the rack to cool completely. "So far, so good."

Trevor ambled into the kitchen, his hair still wet from a shower. His eyes crinkled at the corners as he smiled at her.

Bailey's heart lurched. This was when he was at his most attractive. No cowboy hat, his dark hair wet and carelessly tousled. A bit of scruff on his face. And when he smiled at her, his whole face lit up. She was way too old for puppy love, but that didn't mean Trevor Anderson didn't make her feel like a teenager.

"Why didn't you wake me, darlin'? I told you I'd help." Trevor's arms slid around her and he kissed the tip of her nose. He whispered in her ear, "I had no one to love up this morning and that's just a darn shame."

Well aware her two employees were watching, Bailey blushed and whispered back, "You looked so peaceful, I didn't want to wake you."

Trevor kissed her lips and hugged her. "Well, I'm here now. What can I do?"

There it was. *The Trevor effect.* Tiny flares of heat coursed through her body. Butterflies ascending. Her lady bits dancing. He was perfect.

Jilly smacked Spencer on the arm. "That's what I want. A hot cowboy who melts my socks off."

Spencer rubbed his arm and mumbled, "Yeah, me, too."

Trevor pulled up to the back door of the Hales Corners' Village Hall.

Other cars waited in line, passengers disembarking, carrying baked goods in boxes and other containers. He frowned. "How many entrants are there, again? I thought you said you were competing against nine others. There's got to be twenty or more people carrying something."

Bailey studied the crowd. "There are a couple of different categories. Cakes, breads, cookies, and pastries. Then an overall Showstopper Award. I'm not sure how many actually signed up, but this seems like the right size crowd."

"Well, I hope the judges don't have to taste every single thing or they're going to have a stomachache."

"I guess last year, there were two judges for each category, then they had the mayor and a few others pick the overall winner."

Trevor grunted. "That makes sense." He pulled up to the door. "Let's get your cake unloaded onto the cart and then I'll go park." He looked into the backseat of his truck. "Everything looks good, so we should be okay."

Bailey smiled and pointed at a small cooler. "I've got extra cake and whipped cream in case it's needed."

Trevor turned off the truck and ran around to open her door. Trevor prided himself on being a gentleman, and gentlemen opened doors for ladies. It had been a small concession for Bailey. She was strong and independent, but even she seemed to appreciate a little chivalry.

She smiled at Trevor as he helped her out of his truck.

Trevor grinned. "Let's do this thing." He went to the back of the truck and quickly assembled the cart. Gently, he placed the large cake box on it. "I'm just going to get you through the doorway. I don't want you tripping on that door lip. It looks uneven." He picked up the cart with the cake box on top and carried it to the door, then set it inside the hallway. He stopped at the door and watched as Bailey grabbed the cart and moved it against the wall. "I'll be right back, darlin'."

Trevor went back to his truck and searched for a parking spot near the door. Just as he started pulling into a free spot, a car pulled up behind him, horn blaring. Inside the car, an obviously frustrated woman gestured angrily. He pulled into the space, cut the ignition, and got out of his truck, locking it. The woman jumped out of her car and started screaming obscenities.

Trevor cocked an eyebrow, then tipped his hat and walked away. The woman was as ornery as an unmilked cow. It wasn't as if he'd parked his car in a reserved spot. What the hell was she carping about? Quickly, he rushed into the building. He gazed at Bailey and grinned. "Some woman tried to take my parking space. I was halfway in when she pulled up and started yelling at me. Said it was her space and no motherfucking Texan was going to take it from her." He mock-shivered. "I was lucky she didn't have a gun. She was nuts."

Before Bailey could respond, a white-haired woman dressed in a gray suit stomped through the doorway and hissed at Trevor. "You took my parking space, you . . . you asshole. I had to park on the lawn. If I get a ticket, I'm coming for you." She lifted her foot and kicked him in the leg.

Trevor fell backward and grabbed the wall for support. Something wedged into his thigh and he began falling toward the floor. He heard Bailey scream, and he tried to throw himself away from the cart. Someone grabbed his arm and attempted to steady him, but he hit the cart, hard. "Dammit it to hell . . ." He finally righted himself and slowly turned to look at the disaster he had made of Bailey's cake.

It wasn't there. Was it on the floor? Trevor panicked.

Bailey sighed, and he turned to her. She held the cake box in her arms, her relief evident. "Sorry, I couldn't help. I was protecting my cake." She gazed at him. "Are you hurt?"

"And more importantly, do you want to press charges?"

Trevor looked over his shoulder and his eyes widened.

A deputy sheriff held the struggling woman by the arm. "I'm pretty sure that kick to the shin is assault, especially after that tumble you took."

The woman sputtered, "You can't arrest me, I'm a judge for the holiday baking contest." She glared at Trevor. "And he deserved it. He took my parking place." Her eyes narrowed. "You're lucky I left my thirty-two at home. Otherwise, I'd of shot your tires out."

"That's it." The deputy spun the woman around and cuffed her. As he did, she kicked him. The lawman growled. "Now we can add assaulting an officer to your list of offenses." He tapped the com on his shoulder. "Barnes, where the heck are you? I need some help. Get down to the back door."

The woman stared at the deputy sheriff for a moment. Then she started wailing.

Trevor tried not to chuckle. Even he recognized crocodile tears.

"Oh, stop your bawling, ma'am," the deputy snapped. "I know when I'm being manipulated."

Bailey cleared her throat. "Well, as entertaining as this has been, I need to get my cake upstairs." She reached into her pocket and pulled out a card. "You can reach either of us at that number if you need us to sign anything." She nudged

Trevor. "Come on, hop-a-long."

Trevor straightened the cart and gently took the cake box from Bailey's arms. He centered it on the cart and began rolling toward the elevator up the hall. He passed the deputy sheriff and winked. "Thanks for the assist. Glad to know *crazy* isn't exclusive to Texas."

"Okay, that looks perfect."

Bailey stood back and admired her chocolate peppermint whipped cream cake. It was culinary perfection, covered with sparkling drifts of red and silver glitter on whipped cream. She handed her phone to Taylor. "Take a photo for me, please."

"Don't you want to wait until the judges award you the ribbon?"

"You can take photos of that too, but first, I need to document the cake before someone cuts into it." She sighed. "I'm so glad I brought a repair kit. When I grabbed the cake box off the cart, I didn't realize I smushed part of it."

"God knows what that durn woman would have done if she had gotten her hands on it."

Bailey smirked. "I don't know what category she was supposed to judge, but I would have hated for her to show up here. No way would she have let me win." She grinned at Trevor and shook her head. "You are such a troublemaker." She gazed at the other cakes set up on other tables in the room. There were several Yule Logs, two fruit cakes, a Panettone, a Sticky Pudding, and other cakes decorated with angels, ornaments, and lights. Thus far, she was the only whipped cream cake.

Trevor side-hugged her. "No intentionally. Well, except when I get you naked, wet, and willing."

Bailey stared at him in surprise. "Not something I want

advertised in a room full of strangers." She pulled away from him and stood by her cake. "The judges are coming."

Two men she had never seen before walked into the room. Slowly, they circled the tables, studying each entry. When the judges reached her, she was tempted to curtsy but smiled instead.

The two men walked around the table and stopped. According to the first judge's badge, he was a pastry chef at a nearby high-end hotel. The other was an instructor at the local culinary school. The first judge gestured toward the cake. "This is very tempting. I wonder if it's as light as it looks. Please cut us a sample and tell us about your cake."

Bailey nodded and quickly cut two slices. "Today, I have made for you a chocolate peppermint whipped cream cake.

"The cake is flavored with melted mint chocolates. A vanilla whipped cream and chocolate peppermint mousse are interspersed between alternate layers. The whipped cream layers are lightly dusted with crushed candy canes. The cake is garnished with chocolate dipped mint leaves, and decorated with edible red and silver glitter, as well as more peppermint cane dust."

The other judge frowned. "I hope the candy cane dust doesn't overpower the overall flavor. That would be disastrous. Like eating mint toothpaste."

Bailey's heart dropped. Seriously? They thought she would enter a cake that tasted like toothpaste? "I was careful to use only a light dusting, sir. The chocolate mint used in the cake is fairly mild, so I wanted to enhance that, not overpower it." She handed each judge a plate with cake and a fork. "Please enjoy."

Each judge forked up a bite. As they chewed, they shared a glance, then nodded. Without a word, they set the plates down and moved on to the Sticky Pudding.

Bailey left the plates on the table. Sometimes, judges

returned to compare entries. She watched carefully as they moved around the room. The men possessed great poker faces. They betrayed no reaction to the entries. After taking small bites of everything, the judges left the room.

When they returned, they asked three entrants to step forward with more samples.

Bailey, filled with dismay, knew she had not won. She gazed at Trevor and made a sad face. She could not believe she wasn't even in the top three. Oh God, they hated her cake. Was it that bad?

Trevor moved over to her and took her hand. "If they don't make you the winner, they're just plum crazy. That cake's spectacular and they know it." He nuzzled her. "Best cake I've ever eaten."

The judges left the room again. Moments later, they returned with three ribbons. They moved around the room, awarding third and second-place.

Bailey was confused. Only one entrant in the final three got a ribbon—third place. Second place went to the Sticky Pudding. The judges made a final, dramatic sweep around the room, then stopped in front of her.

The first judge smiled. "After we tasted your cake, nothing else compared."

Bailey sighed with relief. "It didn't taste like toothpaste?"

The judge chuckled. "Not at all. It tasted like Christmas." He picked up his plate and took another bite. "Tell me, what's the secret ingredient? It's heavenly."

"Frango milk chocolate mints."

The man shook his head, still smiling. "Should have known. Marshall Field's. My mother loved those. She put out a box every Christmas. My brothers and I would battle for the last one. You filled this cake with memories. Happy ones." He set down a large blue ribbon next to her cake. "Congratulations. Now the good part. I need you to plate ten slices for the final tasting, for the Showstopper Award. Good luck."

Trevor swept her into a hug. "I knew you had a winner. Congratulations."

Bailey nuzzled him. "Thanks to you. I couldn't have done it without you."

"Well, I was happy to do it with you."

Inwardly, Bailey sighed. Two more weeks. Then he'd be gone.

Chapter Six: Sometimes, Winning Isn't Everything

Spencer skipped into the kitchen and plopped a paper crown from a fast-food restaurant onto Bailey's head.

"I was aiming for a tiara, but the toy stores didn't have any. I guess princesses are big at Christmas."

Bailey rolled her eyes. "Among little girls, princesses are always big." She patted the paper crown. "As tacky as this is, I'll wear it. I feel like a princess." She grinned and squealed. "Oh my God, I won. I won. I can't believe it."

Spencer beamed. "I'm so proud of you, boss. First place in cakes, then the Showstopper Award. Those cakes are going to be all the rage around here. Everyone is going to want one. We are going to be so busy, we'll be baking around the clock." He stopped. "We are going to hire extra help, right?"

Bailey chuckled. "Of course. I just hope I can find enough boxes of the secret ingredient. It's in demand at Christmas. My mother says they used to make them on the thirteenth floor of the Marshall Field's State Street Store in Chicago — for something like seventy years. Now it's outsourced to some place in Pennsylvania. I need to convince them to sell me Frangos in bulk."

"Why not use some other company's mint meltaway? Probably cheaper and less in demand."

Bailey sniffed. "You have no appreciation for history or quality. Frango mints have no equal. They are the perfect combination of mint and chocolate. They transform a chocolate cake from ordinary to extraordinary."

"Nothing's that perfect. Why not ask a chocolatier in town to duplicate it? Or better yet, why not make your own?"

"Ohhh, my poor, disillusioned child. You have so much to learn. Eventually, people are going to beg for the recipe and the more specific I am, the better chance they have of reproducing it. I am perfectly willing to give credit where it's due."

"Oh, oh, I have a better idea. We could do a cookbook featuring your best recipes. Sell it to benefit a local charity. Or maybe include some of those yummy men at the fire station eating your desserts. In a calendar." Spencer flashed a self-satisfied grin. "We could call it something like Butts and Batters, or maybe Pecs and Pastries, or Sweets and Sweats." He shook his hands out. "I'm getting all sweaty just thinking about it."

Bailey laughed. "If you can convince the fire department to participate, I'm all in. Except I don't want them sweating on my sweets." She screwed up her face. "How about Tea with Bailey?"

"Damn, woman. Kill all the joy." He stuck out his bottom lip. "You have a man. Have pity on the rest of us."

Bailey muttered. "For two more weeks, then we're both in the same boat." *Damn.*

Bailey turned off the light, locked the door, and set the alarm. Since winning the baking contest, orders for her Chocolate Peppermint Whipped Cream Cake had been pouring in.

Unfortunately, she could only fulfill orders for twenty-four people. There was no way she was making Spence and Jilly work on Christmas Eve or Christmas. All of them had baked around the clock and they all deserved a break.

If the weather held, she was going to head to Minneapolis to celebrate the holidays with her sisters and brothers and their families. While there was hardly anything restive about spending the holidays with her twelve nieces and nephews, it beat sitting alone in her apartment. At least up north, she wouldn't have time to mourn Trevor's departure. She knew their relationship had an end date, but that didn't make it any easier to say goodbye.

She couldn't deny that she had feelings for him, but that was on her. She had opened her heart to Trevor, and now he was going to break it. As her mother often said, *when you make your bed, you lie in it.*

Tonight would be their last night together. Bailey would insist on it. When she returned from Minneapolis, she needed to move forward. That required a clean break now. No hopes. No dreams. A simple goodbye. At her age, people fell in love, but with marriage and kids out of the equation, break-ups didn't evoke the same emotions. Most of the time. There was no sense of failure or loss. There was only a slight sadness at an impending absence.

Right. Whom did she think she was fooling? She could pretend to be an adult about it, but dammit, all she wanted to do was curl up and cry. That man made her feel alive. He gave each of her days a purpose. He supported her, but he also challenged her. She couldn't think of a more perfect partner. Bailey knew Trevor couldn't stay. Wouldn't stay. He had a life in Texas and she had one here. There was no way either could leave their lives behind.

Bailey emitted a long-suffering sigh. It was useless to hope when there was none. Damn.

She turned from the door and walked to her apartment.

If she was still a child, she'd send a letter to Santa. He always made things right. Too bad adults didn't get the same privilege.

Bailey turned to Trevor and grinned. "This is why you bought me cowboy boots?"

Trevor came up behind her and wrapped his arms around her waist. "I was a bit curious. Bevvy loves this place. Comes here with her girlfriends to hoof it. She claims it's as much fun as a Texas barn dance."

Bailey quickly handed her wrap to the woman at the coat check and pulled Trevor onto the dance floor. After a Two-Step and a Do-Si-Do, they moved into a line dance. Bailey grinned. "I love a good Boot Scootin' Boogie." She stepped out, stepped behind, and stuck out her heel, then repeated the pattern.

Trevor stared at her. "Well, I'll be an egg-sucking dog. You dance like you were born and raised in Texas. Where'd you learn to dance like that, darlin'?"

Bailey smirked and continued line dancing. When the song ended, she stopped and took his hand. She pulled him toward the long bar, apparently constructed from rescued barn doors. "It's been a while, but I won a line dancing competition in law school. One of my friends was from Oklahoma. She taught me well."

Trevor removed his hat and wiped his brow. "You are full of surprises." He nodded across the room at an electronic bull. "And how are you on that?"

Bailey made a face. "My top score was five seconds. Twenty years later, it's probably less than one." She kissed him. "Now I'm too old to try. Those mechanical bulls are for women trying to impress a man or too drunk to care."

Trevor mock-frowned. "You don't want to impress me, darlin'?"

Bailey giggled. "The only bull I intend to ride this evening is you." She laid a hand on his arm and fluttered her eyebrows. "You already know what I can do wearing a cowboy hat."

Trevor choked on his beer. He swiped at his mouth and pulled Bailey close. He lightly tapped her butt and whispered,

"And you know what I can do without one."

And there it was. The heat sizzled up and down her body and settled into her core. Bailey picked up her beer, took a long drink, and set it back on the bar. "As much as I'd love to drag you into a bathroom and have my way with you, I don't fancy a ticket for public indecency. It will have to wait. Let's dance."

Trevor growled and dragged her against him. He lowered his lips to hers and thrust his tongue into her mouth.

Bailey moved closer to him, enjoying the warmth of his roaming hands. Her center rubbed against his rigid cock and she moaned. She lost all sense of time and place as she indulged in Trevor's kiss. Until someone tapped her shoulder. She turned and frowned at an older curvy woman wearing a rhinestone cowboy hat. She had rhinestones everywhere — her shirt, her jeans, and her boots. The woman clucked her tongue and glowered at Bailey. "Hon, we all remember how to do *it*, so we don't need no demonstrating." She gestured at Trevor. "Zip it up and take it home. You're behaving like horny teenagers."

Bailey's mouth dropped open. She gazed at Trevor and stifled a laugh.

With a glint in his eye, Trevor placed his hat on his head and swept Bailey into his arms. "My apologies, ma'am. You see, I just met this filly and I already know I'm going to marry her. I just can't get enough." He nodded and politely said, "All zipped up and headed home." Still carrying Bailey, he moved through the still-dancing crowd.

He glared at the awkward twenty-something who suggested Bailey was drunk and smiled at the young woman who sighed and placed her hands over her heart.

Bailey just reveled in his heat and strength. How the hell was she going to give this man up?

Trevor carried Bailey from his truck into his rented home.

The outside was no longer without decoration. In fact, it now looked like it was competing on one of those TV holiday decorating shows.

Bailey stared at the display and giggled.

"You hush. You're the one who told me to move the lights outdoors." Trevor kicked open the door and while still holding Bailey, he flipped a switch and the fireplace glowed. He hit another switch and the soft lights of the Christmas trees enveloped them. The final switch unleashed romantic music.

Bailey snorted. "God, this place went from a winter wonderland to a playboy's paradise. What did you do?"

"I stuffed some decorations in a closet, moved most of the lights outside, and installed a bunch of dimmer switches. A grown man can only take so much of a daughter's frivolity." He smirked. "No way I could woo a woman when my house looked like a darn carnival sideshow."

Bailey shot him a sultry look. "Are you trying to woo me, cowboy? Not sure that makes much sense since you're leaving in a few days."

Trevor grunted. "Says who? I just bought this house and some land near Franklin. Decided there was nothing here that I wanted to leave behind. Not my daughter, my grandkids, and especially not you." He gently sat Bailey on an over-stuffed leather couch and kneeled to pull off her boots. Then he sat and set her on his lap. "I'm afraid I've become quite fond of you, Bailey Willis. In fact, I love you. It's okay if you're not there yet, but I'm not giving up. I'm an ornery old fool and stubborn as hell. There is no way I'm moving on until you send me on my way."

Bailey's mouth fell open. She stared at Trevor, tears blooming in her eyes. In a voice choked with emotion, she stammered, "I love you, too. I was afraid you were going to leave me behind. Break my heart and two-step back to Texas."

Trevor swiped at her eyes and drew her in for a kiss.

Bailey wrapped her arms around his neck and ran her fingers through his hair. She gazed at him with heat and her lips touched his.

Trevor wanted to cheer. He had fretted all afternoon over what he needed to say. He was sure Bailey was attracted to him, but he wasn't sure she loved him. Bailey was a very independent woman. After she had dismissed relationships, he didn't think love was a possibility. It was a relief that she'd been quick to respond when he professed his love. His heart hadn't been this full since his wife died. He paused. Mariah. He would always love that woman. She had been his life for way too many years. But somehow, he had found room for another and for that, he was grateful.

Bailey snuggled against him and sighed. "Too bad we can't spend Christmas together. I'm afraid I promised my family I'd make the drive to Minneapolis to celebrate with them." She toyed with his belt and gazed at him. "But I can spend New Year's with you."

Trevor hid his chuckle well. His woman was in for a huge Christmas surprise. Thank God he'd had the money to pull it off.

CHAPTER SEVEN: THE END?

The bright sunshine of a freezing winter morning forced Bailey's eyes open.

She stretched, then groaned. The last thing she wanted to do was drive to Minnesota today. Bailey sat up and tiredly pushed herself to her feet. Shower first. Head home, pack, and hit the road.

Trevor grabbed her around the waist and pulled her back into the warm bed. "Where do you think you're going?"

Bailey laughed. "I told you I have to head to Minneapolis. The earlier I leave, the sooner I get there and get off the road before snow or other winter weather hits."

"There's a storm in the forecast? I didn't hear that."

Bailey offered a rueful smile. "In Minnesota, the winter weather changes faster than you change underwear. One minute it's sunny and mild, the next, you get two feet of snow dumped on you. I'm not taking any chances."

"Why not fly? It would be easier."

Bailey shrugged. "I like having a car readily available. When my family gets to be too loud, I can take a drive or leave. With all the kids, family gatherings get crazy, and without earplugs, the noise level wears on me."

Trevor made a strange face. "I see." He pulled closer and kissed her. "Well, before you leave, I insist on buying you breakfast, and then giving you a Christmas gift." He slapped her butt. "Best we get a move on."

Bailey pulled away. "You stay here. I'm taking a shower . . . alone. You get too busy when we shower together and I want to get to my brother's house while it's still day-light."

Trevor harrumphed. "Are you kidding me? Seems like a little shower sex with the one you love should be a guarantee. At least on Christmas Eve."

Bailey shook a finger at him. "Behave." She slipped out of the bed and walked toward the ensuite. "You can shower in the guest room." When Trevor tried to chase her, she slammed the bathroom door and locked it. Trevor made a whimpering noise, but Bailey just snickered. Hurriedly, she showered, dressed, and dried her hair. No way was she heading outdoors with wet hair. Frozen hair was a thing to be avoided in Wisconsin. It wasn't something she aspired to.

When she finished, she unlocked the bathroom door and stepped back into Trevor's bedroom. "Trevor?"

Strong, muscular arms pulled her against a firm chest. Trevor kissed her neck. "Took you long enough. I even started the coffee."

"I thought we were going out." She turned and pecked Trevor on the lips.

He nodded toward the bedstand, where two travel tumblers sat. "I figured we'd need one for the road." Trevor pulled her across the room and handed one to her. "Let's get a move on. We're meeting everyone at the Country Club."

Bailey frowned. "Please tell me we're not going to *Breakfast with Santa*. I don't have time for that. I need to—"

Trevor shut her up with a kiss. "At the risk of sounding like a sexist, there's no need for you to worry your pretty little head about that. You'll see your family soon enough. Come on." He pulled Bailey toward the front door and helped her with her coat, then adorned his own. He opened the front door, where a town car awaited, complete with a chauffeur.

Bailey stared at him. "What in the world?"

Trevor laughed. "I would have rented a sleigh, but I wasn't

in the mood to freeze my nuts off. This seemed like a better option."

The uniformed driver opened the car door and Bailey slid in. She couldn't hide her confusion. Who hired a car to go to breakfast? Bailey studied Trevor. He seemed awfully proud of himself. What was he up to?"

Trevor just patted her hand and kissed her cheek. "Relax, everything will be fine."

Bailey put on her seatbelt and looked out the window, lost in thought. She barely noticed the route they were taking until they passed a sign that said Caledonia, five miles. "Hey, wait a minute. He's gone past the country club." Bailey leaned over and tapped on the glass that separated them from the driver. When the driver ignored her, she turned to Trevor. "This guy doesn't know where he's going.

Trevor stretched out his legs and inspected his nails. "Sure, he does. I gave him a map."

Bailey arched an eyebrow, trying to contain her fury. She did not have time for this. Suddenly, the car slowed and turned into what looked like a driveway. The car pulled into a small circular parking area and stopped at carved wooden doors. Bailey leaned over Trevor and tried to figure out where they were. It looked like some sort of log cabin on steroids. It was huge. "What is this place?"

"Let's go in and check it out."

The chauffeur opened the car door just as the massive front doors opened and a lithe, stylishly dressed blonde woman stepped out. She waved them into the house. "Come on, y'all. It's colder than a frosted frog out here."

Bailey's eyes widened. She grabbed Trevor's hand and whispered, "Who's that?"

"That's Bevvy. I thought you two had met."

"Kind of. I've spoken to her on the phone, but never really met her in person. Why are we at her house? I don't have time for . . . "

"Just shush, now. This is your Christmas present."

Bailey frowned and shook her head.

Trevor chortled. When they stepped through the front door, he mock-whispered, "We'd better move this along, Bevvy. She's getting as ornery as a bull in heat."

Bevvy tittered. "Oh, Daddy. Everyone knows bulls don't go into heat. They just take advantage of it." She nudged a handsome man dressed in an expensive suit who stood next to her. "Isn't that right, Billy darlin'?"

The man smirked. "Never thought I'd have to give my father-in-law a lecture about the birds and the bees." He stuck out a hand to Bailey. "In case you haven't figured it out, this is Bevvy and I'm Bill. You'll meet our kids soon. Right now, they're playing . . ." Bevvy nudged him with an elbow and sent him a dirty look. He stopped speaking and blushed. "Dammit."

Bailey heard the thunder of running feet. "Auntie B, Auntie B. You're finally here." Bailey's five-year-old nephew Zeke threw himself at her and wrapped his arms around her legs. "What took you so long?" He rubbed a hand across his nose and grinned up at her. "Did you bring cookies? Mommy said you'd bring cookies if we were good."

Bailey swallowed. "Zeke?" She bent over and hugged him. "What are you doing here?"

Zeke shrugged. "According to Daddy, some cowboy with more money than brains sent us all tickets to come see you instead." He looked at the adults standing around and pointed at Trevor, who was not wearing his cowboy hat. "Are you a cowboy?" A confused expression crossed his face. "Where's your hat? And your horsie. Cowboys always have horsies."

Bailey gazed at Trevor. Other than the comment about Trevor's wealth—something she had never thought about—she was glad to see her nephew. She arched her eyebrow. "Are you the cowboy with more money than brains?"

Trevor had the decency to blush. "Well, I just thought, given the weather and all, it would be easier to bring your family here. That way, you wouldn't get stuck up there. With a snowstorm or something."

Bevvy laughed. "Daddy, just tell her the truth. It's okay to admit that you didn't want to spend Christmas without her, so you brought her entire family here." She grinned at Bailey. "At first your family thought he was nuts because there's so many of you. But Daddy insisted, and when he puts his mind to it, he always gets his way. So I guess that means he has money and brains."

Bailey's eyes grew wide. "My whole family is here?" She looked around. "Did you stuff them in the closet? They have never been this quiet." Bailey put two fingers between her lips and whistled loudly. Two short bursts, then a long one. Suddenly, the hallway was teeming with her parents and her siblings with their significant others. There were also a multitude of nieces and nephews, most of whom were still in their pajamas. "You guys slept here last night? Is this some sort of AirBnB?"

Her older brother, Randy, shrugged. "Something like that. This place has eight bedrooms. One of them has four bunk beds. Great for a passel of kids." He hugged Bailey. "Wait'll you see the backyard. Now that is truly amazing."

His wife, Candy, pulled him away from Bailey. She moved in for a hug. Candy whispered into Bailey's ear, "I don't know where you found this guy, but holy cow, he's handsome and loaded. Cowboy heaven. Lucky you."

Two little girls with pigtails, twins, tugged on Bailey's sweater. One of them asked, "Auntie B, did you bring our presents? Mommy said you'd have presents."

Bailey kneeled down to their level. She tugged at their

pigtails. "That all depends on whether you're on Santa's naughty list. Remember, he always consults with me on Christmas Eve. I only give presents to little boys and girls on the Nice List, even if I already love them to pieces." She pulled the two girls into her arms and hugged them. "So, Molly and Marie, what will Santa tell me this year?"

Molly shook her head. "I've been really, really good this year." She pointed at Marie. "But she cut the hair off of my Barbie. Now she's practically bald."

Bailey gazed at Marie sternly. She had already heard about the incident and had bought Molly a Barbie Dream House as a gift. Marie would get a talking Barbie book. She and the girl's parents had agreed that the discrepancy was warranted. Marie had not been sufficiently remorseful after the incident. Molly would also receive a new Barbie and lots of Barbie clothing from her parents, while Marie got a Barbie video. It was a tough lesson for a six-year-old, but her parents felt it was too important to overlook. It was not right to destroy other people's property and a half-hearted apology did not compensate for that.

She hugged Molly again. "I'm very sorry that happened to you. When I was your age, my sister Lauren tried to bury my Ken doll in the backyard." She winked at her older sister. "She got in big trouble, too. In fact, I believe Santa gave her coal that year."

All the kids turned to Lauren and stared at her. Lauren's daughter, eight-year-old Mallory, put her hands on her hips and glared at her mother. "Mommy, that's just shameful. You owe Auntie B a big apology, or I'll send you to bed without your supper." She huffed. "You're supposed to set a good example for your children. Just shameful."

Bailey's family burst into laughter and Bailey shook a finger at the chagrinned Lauren. "Yes, just shameful! You still owe me a Ken doll." She giggled and stood. She grabbed

Trevor's hand and kissed him. "Though I may have found me a live version."

Trevor rolled his eyes and chuckled. "Well, thank you, darlin'. There's no bigger compliment than being compared to a male doll without adequate . . . er, equipment." The adults laughed. He gestured to everyone. "Let's go into the dining room, shall we?" He sniffed the air. "I smell pancakes and bacon." His stomach growled as he took Bailey's hand. "I'm ready to eat!"

Zeke grabbed Trevor's other hand and peered up at him hopefully. "I've been really good this year, and I'd really like a horsie." He made a face. "A real one. Not a fake one that just rocks. A real one that poops, and snorts, and everything." His expression turned sly. "Think you can arrange that?"

Trevor grinned. "Are you going to take care of him? Clean out his stall and pick up his sh . . . poop? And feed him and brush him daily? Horses are a lot of work."

Zeke's face fell. "Well, okay. Maybe . . . a puppy?" He smiled. "One that doesn't poop."

Bailey tried not to laugh. *Kids.*

Trevor looked around the great room and smiled.

Bevvy had done a great job at staging the place. There were two gaily decorated Christmas trees with what looked like hundreds of presents underneath each tree. The trees stood in front of large floor-to-ceiling windows. A rustic stone fireplace sat between and was covered with boughs of pine bedecked with bright ribbons. The gas fireplace glowed softly, its flames bouncing off the highly polished floors. Beyond the windows, Bevvy had strung fairy lights in the trees. Although it was daylight, the gray skies of winter offered a suitable background for the multicolored bulbs.

Bailey gazed at Trevor. "This place is gorgeous. How did you find it?"

"Thank Bevvy. This was one of her flip projects. The guy she originally sold it to got transferred overseas. She bought it back from him, improved on some of his wife's changes to the kitchen and bathrooms, and started renting it out short term. Wait'll you see the kitchen? It's commercial grade."

"What's with all the bunks in the one bedroom? Did the guy have a lot of kids?"

"No. Bevvy rented those for your nieces and nephews, and swapped out some of the furniture for stuff more suitable for a large group."

Bailey studied him. "I can't believe you did this. For me. It's kind of overwhelming."

Trevor slid his arm around her waist. "I hope I didn't overstep. Your family was kind of taken aback when I offered to bring them down here and pay for their ride." He stroked his angular chin. "Your dad really fought me. Did not want to accept anything from a stranger. He's a tough cookie."

"You know my father could have paid for this, right?" Her father had several patents to his name for shopping apps. Those had made him incredibly wealthy. Bailey gazed at Bevvy as she and another woman set food on a long picnic table while her brothers and sisters tried to reign in their hungry children. Bill was handing out drinks in sippy cups, as well as traditional glassware. It was pretty obvious that the drink of preference among the adults was a Bloody Mary.

Trevor grunted. "As he informed me, repeatedly." He grasped her chin gently and gazed directly into her eyes. "But this was *my* gift to you, not his. If he had paid for it, it would not have been from me."

"Did he make you grovel?"

"He did, but I don't think he's ever squared off against a Texan. I'm stubborn as a mule when I want something, so he finally conceded."

Bailey moved to the table and sat on an open seat. Trevor

slid in next to her. Two pre-teen girls seated at the opposite end picked up their plates and moved across from him.

"We were waving at you, Grandpa. Didn't you see us?" The young blonde was a carbon copy of Bevvy. The other was several years younger, with her father's steel-gray eyes and brown hair.

Trevor grinned at her. "Evie, you just saw me yesterday. Why would you want to hang out with this old man today when you flirt with some boys?"

Evie blushed. "Oh, Grandpa. I don't have time for boys. They're so silly, sometimes."

The other girl snickered. "She's got her sights set on some basketball player on the middle school team." She stage-whispered, "He's not very good and when he gets off the court, he really stinks."

Evie's eyes shot daggers at her sister. "Mari, Stephen does not stink. Basketball is sweaty work."

Trevor guffawed. "Well, if Stephen has to work at it, he probably stinks — at basketball."

Mari jumped up and high-fived Trevor. She giggled. "Exactly."

Trevor gestured at Bailey. "Girls, this is my sweetheart, Bailey. Bailey, these are my grandkids, Evelyn and Mariah."

Mari smiled. "Nice to meet you. Finally. Grampa talks about you all the time."

Evie studied Bailey, her expression a bit more wary. "Mommy says you own the tea shop that catered my birthday party. The food was decent."

Bailey bit her tongue. Really? Did she forget she had sent a thank you note? "I appreciated your note. It was very sweet."

Evie ignored the comment and stuffed a forkful of pancakes into her mouth.

Mari laughed. "Don't mind her. Mommy says if she's this snotty now, she's going to be hell when she gets her period."

Trevor visibly choked.

Bailey quickly put her hand on his leg to silence him. Tweens were snotty. She'd witnessed that firsthand in her shop. Reprimanding her in any way wouldn't help. Bailey took a bite of her eggs and winked. *Settle down, cowboy.*

After everyone finished breakfast and the table was cleared, Trevor guided Bailey into the kitchen.

Bailey stared in wonder at a beautifully-appointed commercial-grade kitchen. It had everything she had ever wanted. Two wall convection ovens, a multi-burner Viking stove with a flat grill, a large refrigerator-freezer combination, and a double dishwasher. An island housed other standard equipment, including a large farmhouse sink and a marble countertop for rolling dough.

"This is awesome. Was the previous owner a chef?" Bailey was stunned. If she could design a kitchen, this would be it.

"Not sure, but come look at this." Trevor pulled her toward a hallway. "Check out this pantry. It's pretty big." He led her into what resembled a large walk-in closet with shelving on both walls. A wine cooler was installed under a counter and an upright freezer stood at the end. "Think what we could do with all this great space."

Bailey merely nodded. Could she afford a place like this? Would Bevvy consider renting it?

Trevor grabbed her hand and pulled her to a set of patio doors.

Bailey gasped when she saw the backyard. A patio next to the house led to a series of raised plat gardens, a small greenhouse, and several trees. In the distance, there were several other structures — a barn, a small silo, and what looked like a chicken coop. She turned to Trevor. "Is this a farm?"

"Yup. A small one. It's not in operation right now, but it could be by spring. Beyond the barn, there's a small fishing pond that's fed by a creek. The only thing it's missing is a hydroponic garden. But that's an easy fix."

"This is almost exactly what I described to you."

"I know." He grinned at her.

Bailey narrowed her eyes. "Please tell me you didn't buy this place." She punched his arm. "Tell me you didn't buy my dream house."

"Nope. I was waiting for your approval. If we're going to be a couple, it would be pretty rude for me to buy stuff without consulting you. You'd have my head." Trevor took both her hands. "But Bailey, I'm ready to build a life with you. Maybe getting a place seems premature, but we may never get a chance at another place like this. Bevvy wants to sell it, and I think we should buy it."

"How's that going to work? We aren't married, and there is no way I can buy it on my own. Heck, I can't even pay half."

"Then maybe you should let go of all those little timelines in your head and take a leap of faith."

"What?" Bailey palmed her face. What on Earth was he talking about?

"I was going to do this later, but this is as good a time as any." Trevor dropped to his left knee and pulled a small blue box from his pocket.

Bailey shook her head. "I don't think . . . "

"That's a problem, darlin'. You think too much. I knew the minute I saw you, I wanted a life with you. We're not kids anymore. The first chapter of our lives is behind us. It's time for the second. There's no reason to wait. Let's get married and get on with it. We can start here and build the life you've dreamed of." He grinned and stood. "Just say *yes*." He took the ring from the box and held her left hand. "Darlin'?"

Bailey stared at him. Okay, maybe she had her entire life mapped out and maybe she hadn't left room for diversions. And this was a very big diversion. Was this man worth the risk? "But you hate Wisconsin. To you, it's the frozen tundra, a vast wasteland inhabited by Yankees and Packers fans. And you have a ranch in Texas. That's a pretty long commute. You know I can't just up and move."

"I already told you I was staying here. In fact, my boys will be here later today so we can settle everything up. They'll have total responsibility for the ranch." He gazed at Bailey, a patient smile on his face. "Trust me, Bailey. I love you, you love me. There's no disputin' that. Everything else will work out."

Bailey gazed at the Texas-style ring Trevor held. It was pretty. A little big. Kind of fancy, though. She could never wear it while baking . . .

Trevor chuckled. "You're thinking you can't wear this while baking, aren't you?"

Bailey offered a half-smile. "I could wear a wedding band, but this is just too much. I'll wear it for Christmas, but after that, you need to replace it with a plain band."

His smile grew wide. "You're agreein' to get married as soon as possible? Say at New Year's?"

Time to take that leap. Bailey. Hesitantly, she nodded. "Yeah, that'll work." Then she straightened her spine and grinned. "You may be a broken-down cowboy, but you've still got some moves."

Want to make your own Peppermint Chocolate Whipped Cream Cake?

All you need to do is substitute melted Frango mints (or other mint meltaways) for the cocoa in the chocolate cake batter. The ratio for substitution is two tablespoons of melted chocolate for three tablespoons of cocoa. Simply adjust your recipe according.

Interested in making your own bourbon caramel?

There are many recipes available on the Internet. The key is to mix a good bourbon with vanilla in the final step.

ABOUT THE AUTHOR

Award-winning author Seelie Kay writes about lawyers in love.

Writing under a nom de plume, the former lawyer and journalist draws her stories from more than 30 years in the legal world. Seelie's creative pen has resulted in more than twenty tales of contemporary and paranormal romance, and romantic suspense.

Seelie resides in a bucolic exurb outside Milwaukee, WI, where she enjoys opera, the Green Bay Packers, gourmet cooking, organic gardening, and an occasional bottle of red wine.

She is also an MS warrior and ruthlessly battles the disease on a daily basis.

Seelie can be found on most social media, including Twitter, Facebook, Instagram, and TikTok. To subscribe to her newsletter, please visit https://rb.gy/w69pim.